Everyday ENGLiSH

每日一句
生活
英語

國家圖書館出版品預行編目資料

每日一句生活英語／ 雅典英研所編著. -- 初版.

-- 新北市 ：雅典文化, 民106. 08印刷

面 ； 公分. --（英語工具書 ；15）

ISBN 978-986-5753-85-6（18K平裝附光碟片）

1. 英語 2. 會話

805. 188　　　　　　　　　　106009845

英語工具書系列　15

每日一句生活英語

執行編輯／范欣楲

內文排版／王國卿

封面設計／姚恩涵

法律顧問：方圓法律事務所／涂成樞律師

總經銷：永續圖書有限公司

永續圖書線上購物網
www.foreverbooks.com.tw

CVS代理／美璟文化有限公司

TEL：（02）2723-9968

FAX：（02）2723-9668

出版日／2017年08月

雅典文化

出版社

22103　新北市汐止區大同路三段194號9樓之1

TEL　（02）8647-3663

FAX　（02）8647-3660

Phonics 自然發音規則對照表

看得懂英文字卻不會念？還是看不懂也不會念？沒關係，跟著此自然發音規則對照表，看字讀音、聽音拼字，另附中文輔助，你就能念出7成左右常用的英文字喔！

自然發音規則，主要分為子音、母音、結合子音與結合母音這四大組。

◎第1組─子音規則

【b】貝 -bag 袋子	【c】克 -car 車子	【d】的 -door 門
【f】夫 -fat 肥胖的	【g】個 -gift 禮物	【h】賀 -house 房子
【j】這 -joke 笑話	【k】克 -key 鑰匙	【l】樂 -light 燈光
【m】麼 -man 男人 (母音前)	【m】嗯 -ham 火腿 (母音後，閉嘴)	【n】呢 -nice 好的 (母音前，張嘴)
【n】嗯 -can 可以 (母音後)	【p】配 -park 公園	【qu】擴- quiet 安靜
【r】若 -red 紅色	【s】思 -start 開始	【t】特 -test 測驗
【v】富 -voice 聲音	【w】握 -water 水	【x】克思 -x-ray x 光
【y】意 -yes 是的	【z】日 -zoo 動物園	

◎第2組─母音規則

短母音		
【a】欨(嘴大) -ask 詢問	【e】欨(嘴小) -egg 蛋	【i】意 -inside 裡面
【o】啊 -hot 熱的	【u】餓 -up 向上	
長母音		
【a】欨意 -aid 幫助	【e】意 -eat 吃	【i】愛 -lion 獅子
【o】歐 -old 老的	【u】物 -you 你	

◎第3組—結合子音規則

【ch】去 -chair 椅子	【sh】噓 -share 分享	【gh】個 -ghost 鬼
【ph】夫 -phone 電話	【wh】或 -what 什麼	【rh】若 -rhino 犀牛
【th】思 -thin 瘦的 (伸出舌頭，無聲)	【th】日 -that 那個 (伸出舌頭，有聲)	【bl】貝樂 -black 黑的
【cl】克樂 -class 班級	【fl】夫樂 -flower 花朵	【gl】個樂 -glass 玻璃
【pl】配樂 -play 玩耍	【sl】思樂 -slow 慢的	【br】貝兒 -break 打破
【cr】擴兒 -cross 橫越	【dr】桌兒 -dream 夢	【fr】佛兒 -free 自由的
【gr】過兒 -great 優秀的	【pr】配兒 -pray 祈禱	【tr】綽兒 -train 火車
【wr】若 -write 寫字	【kn】呢 -know 知道	【mb】嗯(閉嘴) -comb 梳子
【ng】嗯(張嘴) -sing 唱歌	【tch】去 -catch 捉住	【sk】思個 -skin 皮膚
【sm】思麼 -smart 聰明	【sn】思呢 -snow 雪	【st】思的 -stop 停止
【sp】思貝 -speak 說話	【sw】思握 -sweater 毛衣	

◎第4組—結合母音規則

【ai】欸意 -rain 雨水	【ay】欸意 -way 方式	【aw】歐 -saw 鋸子
【au】歐 -sauce 醬汁	【ea】意 -seat 座位	【ee】意 -see 看見
【ei】欸意 -eight 八	【ey】欸意 -they 他們	【ew】物 -new 新的
【ie】意 -piece 一片	【oa】歐 -boat 船	【oi】喔意 -oil 油
【oo】物 -food 食物	【ou】澳 -outside 外面	【ow】歐 -grow 成長
【oy】喔意 -boy 男孩	【ue】物 -glue 膠水	【ui】物 -fruit 水果
【a_e】欸意 -game 遊戲	【e_e】意 -delete 刪除	【i_e】愛 -side 邊、面
【o_e】歐 -hope 希望	【u_e】物 -use 使用	【ci】思 -circle 圓圈
【ce】思 -center 中心	【cy】思 -cycle 循環	【gi】句 -giant 巨人
【ge】句 -gentle 溫和的	【gy】句 -gym 體育館	【ar】啊兒 -far 遠的
【er】兒 -enter 輸入	【ir】兒 -bird 小鳥	【or】歐兒 -order 順序
【ur】兒 -burn 燃燒	【igh】愛 -high 高的	【ind】愛嗯的 -find 找到

現在你可以運用上述自然發音的規則，試念以下這些句子：

★ Anything wrong?

★ It's time for bed.

★ Let's go for a ride.

★ May I use the phone?

★ Nice to meet you.

★ That sounds good.

★ I feel thirsty.

★ Turn off the light, please.

★ May I leave now?

★ Here you are.

Chapter 1 一般對話常用問句

1. Anybody home?
有人在家嗎？ 034

2. Anything else?
還有其他問題嗎？ 034

3. Any messages for me?
有我的留言嗎？ 035

4. Are you crazy?
你瘋了嗎？ 036

5. Are you kidding?
你在開玩笑嗎？ 037

6. Are you married?
你結婚了嗎？ 038

7. Are you seeing someone?
你最近有心儀的人嗎？ 038

8. Are you serious?
你是認真的嗎？ 039

9. Are you sure?
你確定嗎？ 040

10. Are you ready?
你準備好了嗎？ 041

11. Can I take a rain check?
我可以改期嗎？ 042

12. Can you speak up?
你可以說大聲一點嗎？ 042

13. Could you do me a favor?
你能幫我一下嗎？ 043

14. Do I have to?
我一定要這麼做嗎？ 044

15. Do you have the time?
現在幾點？ 045

16. Do you have time?
你有空嗎？ 046

17. Do you mind？
你介意嗎？ 046

18. Do you drink?
你喝酒嗎？ 047

19. Does it work?
那有用嗎？ 048

20. Don't you know?
你不知道嗎？ 049

21. Feel better?
有好點嗎？ 050

22. Guess what?
猜猜看？ 051

23. How about that?
你覺得那個如何呢？ 052

24. How can you say that?
你怎麼可以這樣說？ 052

25. How come?
為什麼？ 053

26. How could you do this to me?
你怎麼可以這樣對我呢？ 054

27. How do you feel?
你感覺如何？ 055

28. How long does it take?
那要花多久的時間？ 056

29. How much?
多少錢？ 056

30. How've you been lately?
最近過得如何？ 057

31. How's it going?
一切都還好嗎？ 058

32. Is it true or false?
這是對的還是錯的？ 059

33. Is that clear?
這樣清楚嗎？ 060

34. Is that so?
是這樣嗎？ 060

35. Is that yours?
那是你的嗎？ 061

36. Is there anything wrong?
有什麼問題嗎？ 062

37. May I?
我可以嗎？ 063

38. May I ask some questions?
我可以問幾個問題嗎？ 064

39. May I help you?
我可以幫你嗎？ 064

40. Really?
真的嗎？ 065

41. So what?
那又如何？ 066

42. That can't be right, can it?
那不可能是對的，是嗎？ 067

43. What are you doing?
你在做什麼？ 068

44. What can I do for you?
我可以幫你什麼嗎？ 068

45. What day is today?
今天星期幾？ 069

46. What did you say?
你剛說什麼？ 070

47. What do you do?
你是做什麼工作？ 071

48. What do you mean?
你是指什麼意思？ 071

49. What do you want?
你想怎麼樣？ 072

50. What does it do?
這個有甚麼用？ 073

51. What does that mean?
那是什麼意思？ 074

52. What happened?
發生什麼事？ 075

53. What have I done?
我做了什麼？ 075

54. What's new?
有什麼新鮮事？ 076

55. What's the meaning of this?
這是什麼意思？ 077

56. What's up?
有什麼事嗎？ 078

57. What's wrong?
怎麼了？ 079

58. What's your problem?
你是怎麼回事啊？ 080

59. What should I do?
我該怎麼辦？ 081

60. What were you thinking?
你在想什麼啊？ 082

61. What would you like?
你想要什麼？ 082

62. What would you say?
你覺得怎樣？ 083

63. Who do you think you are?
你以為你是誰？ 084

64. Who do you think you are talkin to?
你以為你在跟誰說話？ 085

65. Who's calling?
是哪一位？ 086

66. Who knows?
誰知道？ 086

67. Who says?
誰說的？ 087

68. Who told you that?
誰告訴你的？ 088

69. Whose turn?
輪到誰？ 089

70. Which would you prefer?
你喜歡哪一個？ 090

71. Why not?
為什麼不呢？/有何不可？ 091

Chapter 2 一般對話常用答句

72. A one-way ticket, please.
請給我一張單程票。 094

73. After you!
你先請！ 094

74. All right!
好吧！/好的。/很好，沒事。 095

75. Any day will do.
哪一天都行。 096

76. As above.
如前述所言/同上。 097

77. ASAP(= As soon as possible)
儘快 098

78. Be careful!
小心！ 098

79. Be my guest.
我請你。 099

80. Be quiet.
安靜。 100

81. Behave yourself.
檢點些吧！ 101

82. Believe it or not!
信不信由你! 101

83. Bingo!
你猜對了！ 102

84. Bottoms up!
乾杯！ 103

85. Call me.
打給我。 104

86. Certainly!
當然！ 105

87. Check it out!
去看一看吧！ 105

88. Come on!
來吧！ 106

89. Control yourself!
克制一下! 107

90. Count me in.
算我一份。 108

91. Easy come, easy go.
來得容易，去得也快。 108

92. Excuse me.
對不起，你可以再說一次嗎？/借過。 109

93. Face the music.
面對現實。 110

94. Fasten your seat belt.
繫好你的安全帶。 111

95. First come, first served.
先到先得。 112

96. Follow me.
跟我來。 112

97. Forget it.
算了。 113

98. Get over yourself.
別自以為是。 114

99. Get to the point.
說重點。 115

100. Go ahead.
你請便。/去做吧！ 116

101. Go straight.
直走。 116

102. Good news.
好消息。 117

103. Haste makes waste.
欲速則不達。 118

104. He always talks big.
他總是吹牛。 119

105. He came by bus.
他搭公車來。 120

106. He is just a child.
他只是個孩子。 120

107. He is looking for a job.
他在找工作。 121

108. He is my age.
他跟我同歲。 122

109. Help yourself.
自行取用。 123

110. Here comes the bus.
公車來了。 123

111. Here you are.
給你。 124

112. Hold on.
等一下！ 125

113. Hurry up!
快一點！ 126

114. I'm fine.
我很好，沒事。 127

115. I'm full.
我飽了。 127

116. I'm home.
我到家了。 128

117. I'm in a hurry!
我在趕時間! 129

118. I'm lost.
我迷路了。 130

119. I'm not sure.
我不確定。 131

120. I'm on a diet.
我在節食。 131

121. I'm single.
我單身。 132

122. I could hardly speak.
我簡直說不出話來。 133

123. I doubt it.
我懷疑。 134

124.I have the right to know.
我有權知道。 135

125. I get the picture.
我明白了。 136

126.I have a runny nose.
我一直流鼻水。 136

127. I have a surprise for you.
我有一個驚喜要給你。 137

128. I have no choice.
我別無選擇。 138

129. I love this game.
我愛這遊戲。 139

130. I made it!
我做到了！ 140

131. I promise.
我保證。 140

132. I quit.
我不幹了。 141

133. I think so.
我也這麼想。 142

134. I've got to go.
我該走了。 143

135. It depends.
那要看情況。 143

136. It hurts.
(傷口)疼。 144

137. It matters a lot to me.
那對我很重要。 145

138. It really takes time.
這樣太耽誤時間了。 146

139. It's a deal!
一言為定！ 146

140. It's a long story.
說來話長。 147

141. It's a piece of cake.
那真是輕而易舉。 148

142. It's getting cold.
變冷了。 149

143.It's raining cats and dogs.
下大雨。 150

144.It's too good to be true!
好得難以置信。 151

145.It's up to you.
看你的決定囉！ 151

146.It's your turn.
輪到你。 152

147.I'll be along later.
我隨後就到。 153

148.I'll be right there.
我馬上就到。 154

149.I'll be back soon.
我馬上回來。 154

150.I'll do my best.
我會盡力而為。 155

151.I'll fix you up.
我會幫你打點的。 156

152.I'll take this please.
我要這個。 157

153.I'll think about it.
我會想一想。 157

154.I'll think it over.
我會好好考慮的。 158

155. Just between you and me.
這是我們之間的秘密。 159

156.Keep in touch!
常保連絡。 160

157.Let's call it a day.
今天到此為止吧。 161

158.Let's get started.
開始幹活吧！ 161

159. Let's see.
讓我們看看。 162

160. Let's take a break.
我們休息一下。 163

161. Life is short.
人生苦短。 164

162. Like father like son.
有其父必有其子。 164

163. Make yourself at home.
甭客氣。 165

164. Me, too.
我也是。 166

165. Money talks.
有錢能使鬼推磨。 167

166. Move forward!
往前進。 167

167. My mouth is watering.
我要流口水了。 168

168. My treat.
我請客。 169

169. Never mind.
沒關係。 170

170. No kidding.
我是說真的。 171

171. No pain no gain.
不勞而無獲。 171

172. No problem!
沒問題！ 172

173. Not yet.
還沒。 173

174. Of course.
當然。 174

175.One more chance, please.
請再給我一次機會。 174

176.One more time.
再一次。 175

177.Practice makes perfect.
熟能生巧。 176

178.Raise your hand, please.
請舉手。 177

179.Read my lips.
你給我仔細聽好了。 178

180.Right now!
就是現在！ 179

181.See you.
再見。 179

182.Seeing is believing.
眼見為憑。 180

183.She has a long face.
她的臉很臭。 181

184.Slow down.
慢一點。 182

185.So do I.
我也是。 183

186.So far so good.
目前為止一切都還好。 183

187.Sorry to interrupt you.
抱歉打擾你。 184

188.Suit yourself.
隨便你。 185

189.Take a look.
看一下。 186

190.Take care.
保重。 186

191.Thanks a lot.
多謝。 187

192.That's all I need.
我就要這些。 188

193.That's it.
夠了。/就是這樣了。 189

194.That's 3the stupidest thing I've ever heard!
那是我聽到的最愚蠢的事！ 190

195.That's your problem.
那是你的問題。 190

196.That makes no difference.
沒什麼差別。 191

197.The answer is zero.
白忙了。 192

198.The price is reasonable.
價格還算合理。 193

199.Things are getting better.
情況正在好轉。 194

200.Think twice.
三思而後行。 194

201.This way.
往這邊。 195

202.Time flies.
時光飛逝。 196

203.Time is money.
時間就是金錢。 197

204.Time's up!
時間到！ 198

205.To go.
外帶 198

206.Try again.
再試一次。 199

207. Turn on the light.
開燈。 200

208. Turn right.
右轉。 201

209. Wait a minute.
等一下！ 201

210. Wake up!
醒來！/起床！ 202

211. Whatever.
無所謂。 203

212. What a nice day it is!
今天天氣真好! 204

213. Yes, I see.
是的，我懂了。 205

214. You are a chicken.
你是個膽小鬼。 205

215. You are just in time.
你來得正是時候。 206

216. You asked for it.
這是你自找的。 207

217. You're all alike.
你們都是一丘之貉。/你們是同一夥的。 208

218. You're so careless.
你真粗心。 208

219. You can call me any time.
你可以隨時打電話給我。 209

220. You've got to do something.
你必須想個法子。 210

221. You need to see a doctor.
你該去看醫生。 211

222. You need a workout.
你需要去運動鍛鍊一下。 212

223. You never change.
江山易改，本性難移。 213

224. You owe me one.
你欠我一個人情。 214

Chapter 3 表達身心情緒狀態用句

225. Cut it out.
省省吧。/停止，別鬧了。 216

226. Don't be that way!
別那樣！ 216

227. Don't bother me!
別煩我！ 217

228. Don't give me that!
少來這套! 218

229. Don't go too far.
別太過分。 219

230. Don't nag me!
別對我碎碎唸！ 220

231. Don't talk to me like that!
別那樣和我說話！ 220

232. Don't touch me!
別碰我！ 221

233. Get lost.
滾開！ 222

234. Get off my case.
別管我。 223

235. Get out of my face!
從我面前消失！ 223

236. Give me a break.
饒了我吧。 224

237. How dare you!
你敢！ 225

238.I'm all in.
我累到筋疲力竭。 226

239.I'm all thumbs!
我真是笨手笨腳！ 226

240.I'm fed up with my work!
我受夠我這個工作了! 227

241.I'm so sorry.
我很抱歉。 228

242.I'm what I am.
我就是我。 229

243.I can't take it anymore!
我受不了了！ 230

244.I don't want to hear it!
我不想聽！ 230

245.   I do.
我願意。 231

246.I got goose bumps.
我都起雞皮疙瘩了。 232

247.I hate you!
我討厭你！ 233

248.I have a headache.
我頭痛。 234

249.I have a stomache.
我肚子痛。 234

250.I have a toothache.
我牙齒痛。 235

251.I've lost my appetite.
我沒食慾。 236

252.I love you!
我愛你！ 237

253.It's incredible!
真是不可思議! 237

254. It's amazing!
真是太令人驚訝了！ 238

255. It surprised me.
那事使我頗感驚訝。 239

256. I'll never forgive you!
我永遠都不會原諒你！ 240

257. Just wait and see!
等著瞧! 241

258. Knock it off.
少來這一套。/別鬧了。 241

259. Leave me alone.
走開。 242

260. Let go.
放手。 243

261. Look at this mess!
看看這爛攤子！ 244

262. Look what you've done!
看看你都做了些什麼！ 245

263. Mind your own business.
少管閒事。 246

264. My God!
我的天哪！ 246

265. Shame on you!
你真是丟臉！ 247

266. Shut up!
閉嘴！ 248

267. Stop complaining!
別發牢騷！ 249

268. Stop fooling around!
別再混了！ 249

269. Take a hike!
哪兒涼快哪兒歇去吧！ 250

270.That's it!
夠了！/就是這樣了！ 251

271.That's terrible!
真糟糕！ 252

272.What a pity!
真是可惜！ 253

273.What the heck!
管它的! 254

274.What a shame !
真可惜！ 255

275.Watch out!
當心！ 256

276.You're a jerk!
你這個混蛋！ 257

277.You crack me up.
你把我笑死了。 257

278.You crossed the line.
你太過分了。 258

279.You deserve it!
活該！/你應得的！ 259

280.You have a lot of nerve.
你臉皮真厚。 260

281.You make me sick!
你真讓我感到噁心！ 261

282.You piss me off.
你氣死我了。 262

283.You set me up!
你出賣我！ 262

284.You're headed for trouble.
你會惹上麻煩。 263

Chapter 4 表達支持、讚美或安慰用語

285. Cheer up!
振作點！ 266

286. Congratulations!
恭喜！ 266

287. Don't give up!
別放棄！ 267

288. Don't sweat it!
別緊張！ 268

289. Don't take it so hard.
別看得太嚴重。 269

290. Don't worry.
別擔心。 270

291. Don't yell at me!
別對我大吼大叫！ 270

292. Enjoy yourself!
祝你玩得開心！ 271

293. Give it a try!
試看看吧！ 272

294. God bless you!
願上帝保佑你！ 273

295. Good luck!
祝你好運！ 274

296. Grow up!
成熟點吧！ 274

297. Have a good time!
玩得愉快啊！ 275

298. I'm on your side.
我支持你。 276

299. I'm proud of you!
我以你為榮！ 277

300.I agree.
　　我同意。 278

301.I can't agree with you more.
　　我非常同意你說的。 278

302.I just want to help you.
　　我只想幫你而已。 279

303.I know you can do it.
　　我相信你可以的。 280

304.Indeed.
　　的確。 281

305.It's worth a try.
　　值得一試。 281

306.Just do it!
　　做就是了。 282

307.Keep it up!
　　堅持下去！ 283

308.Keep the change.
　　不用找了。 284

309.Keep your pants on.
　　沉住氣，忍耐點。 284

310.Let it be!
　　就讓它去吧！ 285

311.Not bad.
　　還不賴。 286

312.Seize the time.
　　把握時間。 287

313.Take it easy.
　　放輕鬆。 288

314.Take your time.
　　別急，慢慢來。 288

315.Thank you for your advice.
　　謝謝你的建議。 289

316.That's a good idea.
那真是個好主意。 290

317.That's so kind of you.
你真好。 291

318.That sounds great!
那聽起來不錯啊！ 292

319.Well done!
做得好！/全熟。 292

320.You're looking sharp!
你看上去真棒。 293

321.You bet!
你說得對！ 294

322.You did a good job.
你做得非常好。 295

323.You did right.
你做得對。 296

324.You have my word.
我會遵守承諾。 296

325.You impress me!
你讓我印象深刻！ 297

326.You really helped me out!
你真的幫了我！ 298

Chapter 5 表達否定、拒絕或命令之意用語

327.Don't be a stranger.
別裝不熟。 300

328.Don't be so childish.
別幼稚了。 300

329.Don't be so mean!
別太尖酸刻薄。 301

330.Don't beat around the bush.
別拐彎抹角。 302

331.Don't fall for it!
別上當! 303

332.Don't fish in troubled water.
別混水摸魚。 304

333.Don't judge a person by his appearance.
別以貌取人。 305

334.Don't let me down.
別讓我失望。 306

335.Don't look at me like that.
別那樣看著我。 306

336.Don't look down on me.
別看不起我。 307

337.Don't make fun of me.
別開我玩笑。 308

338.Don't move!
不准動！ 309

339.Don't waste your breath.
別浪費力氣了。 310

340.I'm not interested.
我沒興趣。 310

341.I'm not sure I can do it.
這事我恐怕做不了。 311

342.I can't afford it.
我負擔不起。 312

343.I can't help it.
我沒辦法。 313

344.I can't wait!
我已經等不及了！ 313

345.I decline.
我拒絕。 314

346.I didn't mean it.
我不是故意的。 315

Chapter 1

一般對話常用問句

1. Anybody home?

有人在家嗎？

說　明

當你按完門鈴或敲完門後，仍無人回應時，即可用此句。另外，若你是與家人或親友同住的情況下，當你回到家時，想知道家裡是否還有其他人時，也可以用這句話來表達。

情境對話1：

Ⓐ (Knock! Knock! Knock!) Anybody home?
(叩！叩！叩！)有人在家嗎？

Ⓑ Yes! Wait a second, please. I'm coming.
有，請等一下，我馬上來。

情境對話2：

Ⓐ I'm home, Mom. (No one answers.)
媽，我到家了。(無人回應)

Ⓐ Anybody home?
有人在家嗎？

字彙：

knock 敲門聲	wait a second 等一下
please 請	come 來
home 家	answer 回答

2. Anything else?

還有其他問題嗎？

說　明

適用於敘述完一件事情或問題之後，若欲詢問對方是否還有疑問時，即可用此句來表達。若之後欲加所陳述之問題，常接 about，例如：Anything else about the question?

情境對話1：

Ⓐ Anything else about the issue today?
關於今天的議題還有其他問題嗎？

Ⓐ If no, the meeting is coming to an end now.
如果沒有，那會議就到此告一段落。

情境對話2：

Ⓐ So, let's adopt the resolution to this project.
那麼，針對這項方案，我們就採取此解決方式。

Ⓐ Anything else about the resolution? Everyone?
關於此解決方式，各位還有其他問題嗎？

字彙：

issue 議題   meeting 會議
come to an end 結束   adopt 採取；接受

3. Any messages for me?

有我的留言嗎？

說　明

通常此問句會應用在辦公室中。當你外出回來後，欲知是否有人來電時，即可問你的同事或助理 Any messages for me?或者，當你在外回家後，也可用此句詢問你的家人，是否有人來電或留話給你。

情境對話1：

Ⓐ Sally, any messages for me?
莎莉，有我的留言嗎？

Ⓑ Yes, here is the note.
有，紙條在這裡。

情境對話2：

Ⓐ Any messages for me, Mom?
媽，有我的留言嗎？

Ⓑ No, not at all.
沒有，一通都沒有。

字彙：

message 訊息、消息	for 給
not at all 一點也不(沒有)	note 便條紙；筆記、紀錄

4. Are you crazy?

你瘋了嗎？

說　明

　當對方說出或做出一些令你感到難以理解或訝異的言行舉動時，就可以用此句表達你的感受。

情境對話1：

Ⓐ I want to explode the company.
我想炸毀那間公司。

Ⓑ Are you crazy?
你瘋了嗎？

情境對話2：

Ⓐ Are you crazy? The typhoon is coming!
你瘋了嗎？颱風要來了耶！

Ⓑ But I still want to go mountain climbing.
但我還是想去登山。

字彙：

explode 爆炸   company 公司
typhoon 颱風   still 仍然
mountain climbing 爬山

5. Are you kidding?

你在開玩笑嗎？

說 明

　當你開始相信對方所說的話,但對方所說的話實在令人難以相信時,就可以用這句話要求對方再加解釋。另外,kidding是口語常用字,只能用在朋友間,不太適合正經的場合使用。

情境對話1：

Ⓐ Are you kidding? You really want to marry that guy?
你在開玩笑嗎？你真的要嫁給那傢伙？

Ⓑ No, I'm not kidding. I really love him.
不,我不是開玩笑。我是真的愛他。

情境對話2：

Ⓐ I think we can start a business together.
我想我們可以一起創業。

Ⓑ Are you kidding? I don't even have a job now!
你在開玩笑嗎？我現在連個工作都沒有！

字 彙

marry 娶；嫁；結婚   guy 傢伙
business 生意；企業   even 甚至

6. Are you married?

你結婚了嗎？

說　明

當你想知道對方是否結婚了沒，或是懷疑對方是否真的結了婚時，就可以用此句表達。

情境對話1：

Ⓐ Are you married?
你結婚了嗎？

Ⓑ No, I'm still single.
不，我仍單身中。

情境對話2：

Ⓐ Really? You are married?
真的嗎？你結婚了？

Ⓑ Yes, of course. Why do you ask me that?
當然。為什麼這樣問我呢？

Ⓐ Because you look so young.
因為你看起來很年輕。

字　彙

single 單身的　　　　　　ask 問
because 因為　　　　　　young 年輕的

7. Are you seeing someone?

你最近有心儀的人嗎？

說　明

當你想知道對方是否在談戀愛，或是發覺自己喜歡的人好像有了交往的對象時，就可以用此句表達。

情境對話 1：

Ⓐ Are you seeing someone?
你最近有心儀的人嗎？

Ⓑ Yes, I'm dating with Peter.
是啊，我正跟彼得交往中。

Ⓐ Oh, that Peter! Now, I remember.
噢，那個彼得啊！現在我記得了。

情境對話 2：

Ⓐ You look different. Are you seeing someone?
你看起來不一樣了。你最近有心儀的人嗎？

Ⓑ No. I just changed my hair style.
沒有啊！我只是換了髮型而已。

字　彙

date 約會　　　　　　　remember 記住
different 不一樣的　　　style 造型

8.　Are you serious?

你是認真的嗎？

說　明

當你質疑對方是否真會執行他自己所說的事情時，而此事也讓你覺得對方有可能會這麼做時，就可以用此句表達。

情境對話 1：

Ⓐ I plan to leave for Africa next month.
我打算下個月要去非洲。

Ⓑ Are you serious? It's really far away from here!
你是認真的嗎？非洲離這裡真的很遠！

情境對話2：

Ⓐ Are you serious? Do you really want to do that?
你是認真的嗎？你真的想這麼做嗎？

Ⓑ Yes! I really do.
是的！我是真的這麼想。

字　彙

plan 計畫；打算	leave for 前往
Africa 非洲	next 下一個
month 月份	far away 很遠

9. Are you sure?

你確定嗎？

說　明

當你想確認對方是否對自己所說的話有充分的把握時，或是想滅滅對手的氣勢，而讓他也懷疑自己的能力時，就可以用此句表達。

情境對話1：

Ⓐ Are you Derek's girlfriend?
你是德瑞克的女朋友嗎？

Ⓑ Yes, I am.
是的，我是。

Ⓐ Are you sure? I saw him with another girl last Friday.
你確定嗎？上星期五我看見他和另一個女生在一起。

情境對話2：

Ⓐ Are you sure that you can beat him in this contest?
你確定你可以在這次比賽中贏過他嗎？

B Definitely! I'm fully prepared for the contest this time.
當然！這次比賽我有充分的準備。

字　彙

beat 打擊；打敗、勝過　　　definitely 絕對地；肯定地
contest 競賽

10. Are you ready?

你準備好了嗎？

說　明

　　此句通常使用在比賽前，或在進行一項活動或執行行動時，用來提醒或者詢問對方是否真的下定決心來做此事，或是否有充分的準備、能力來面對挑戰的情況時，就可以用此句來表達。

情境對話1：

A Are you ready?
你準備好了嗎？

B Well, I am not sure. Maybe I still need more time.
我不太確定。也許我還是需要多一點時間。

情境對話2：

A Are you ready for this job?
你準備好要做這份工作了嗎？

B Yes, I am ready.
是的，我準備好了。

字　彙

maybe 也許　　　　　　　need 需要
more 更多　　　　　　　　job 工作；職業

11. Can I take a rain check?

我可以改期嗎？

說　明

當對方跟你約定好日期和時間後，但你突然發現無法如期赴約時，就可以跟對方說這句話來延後日期或改期。或者是詢問你在某個時間一起去參加一個活動，但你不太想去，卻又不好意思直接婉拒時，也可以用此句表示。

情境對話1：

Ⓐ How about going to see a movie tomorrow?
不然明天我們去看電影，你覺得呢？

Ⓑ Sorry! I have to work tomorrow. Can I take a rain check?
不好意思！我明天要上班。我可以改期嗎？

情境對話2：

Ⓐ Hey, let's go fishing this Friday night!
嘿，這星期五晚上我們去夜釣！

Ⓑ Can I take a rain check? I need to accompany my child that day.
我可以改期嗎？我那天要陪我的小孩。

字　彙

movie 電影　　　　　　go fishing 釣魚
accompany 陪同

12. Can you speak up?

你可以說大聲一點嗎？

說　明

當對方講話的音量過小或讓你聽不見時，就可以跟他說這句話。

情境對話1：

Ⓐ Can you please speak up so we can hear you?
你可以説大聲一點嗎？這樣我們才聽得到你在説什麼。

Ⓑ Ok!
好！

情境對話2：

Ⓐ Can you speak up? It's very noisy here.
你可以説大聲一點嗎？這裡很吵。

Ⓑ I said, "You forgot to put on your shoes!"
我説，你忘了穿鞋子！

字　彙

hear　聽見　　　　　　　　　noisy　吵雜的

forgot (forget 的過去式) 忘記　put on　穿上

shoe　鞋子

13. Could you do me a favor?

　　你能幫我一下嗎？

說　明

　當你需要別人幫忙時，就可以使用此句。另外，也有人會説 Can you do me a favor？或是 Can you help me？但相較之下，Could you do me a favor？是比較有禮貌，也會讓對方感覺到你尊重他的用法。

情境對話1：

Ⓐ Could you do me a favor? I can't find my purse.
你能幫我一下嗎？我找不到我的錢包。

Ⓑ Ok. I found it! It's over there!
好。我找到了！它在那裡！

情境對話2：

Ⓐ Could you do me a favor and lend me ten thousand dollars?

你能幫我一下，借我一萬塊好嗎？

Ⓑ I'm not sure I have enough money to lend you.

我不確定我有足夠的錢借你。

字　彙

find 尋找	purse 錢包(女用)
lend 借	thousand 千
dollar 元	enough 足夠的

14. Do I have to?

我一定要這麼做嗎？

說　明

當對方要求或請求你做一件你不太願意做的事情時，就可以用此句表達，讓對方知道其實你不是真的想幫他做該事。但一般情況下，你還是得幫對方這個忙。

情境對話1：

Ⓐ Do I have to do this? It's embarrassing.

我一定要做這件事嗎？那會很尷尬！

Ⓑ Yes! You have to.

是的！你一定得這麼做。

情境對話2：

Ⓐ Do I have to go home now? The party is so fun!

我一定得現在回家嗎？那個派對很有趣耶！

Ⓑ Yes! For your own good!

是的！為了你好！

字　彙

embarrassing 尷尬的　　　　party 派對；舞會
fun 有趣、好玩的

15. Do you have the time?

現在幾點？

說　明

當你想知道時間，卻沒有戴手錶或手機時，就可以問別人 Do you have the time？也可以說 What time is it？

情境對話1：

Ⓐ Excuse me. Do you have the time, please?
不好意思。請問現在幾點？

Ⓑ It's six-thirty p.m.
現在是晚上六點半。

情境對話2：

Ⓐ Kenny, do you have the time? I need to catch the train at ten o'clock.
肯尼，現在幾點了？我必須趕上十點的火車。

Ⓑ Oops! Only ten minutes left now! Let me drive you there!
哎喲!現在只剩十分鐘了！我開車載你去吧！

字　彙

thirty 三十　　　　　　catch 抓住；趕上
train 火車　　　　　　minute 分鐘
left 剩餘的　　　　　　drive 開車

16. Do you have time?

你有空嗎？

說　明

　當你想問對方有沒有空時，就可以用這句話，也可以用 Are you free？來問別人。另外加不加 the，意思就不同了，加 the，就是問對方現在幾點的意思。

情境對話1：

Ⓐ Sam, do you have time now?
　山姆，你現在有空嗎？

Ⓑ Sure!
　當然有空！

情境對話2：

Ⓐ Mom, do you have time to help me with Kelly this Saturday?
　媽，這個星期六你有空幫我照顧凱莉嗎？

Ⓑ Well, can I say no?
　我可以說不嗎？

字　彙

help 幫忙

17. Do you mind?

你介意嗎？

說　明

　當你覺得自己所要做的事情，不知道是否會引起別人的反感或不悅時，就可以用這句話表示。

情境對話1：

Ⓐ I feel so hot! Do you mind opening the window?
我覺得好熱！你介意我打開窗戶嗎？

Ⓑ No, not at all.
不，一點也不。

情境對話2：

Ⓐ Do you mind if I smoke?
你介意我抽菸嗎？

Ⓑ Certainly! Don't you see the sign"No smoking!" on the wall?
當然介意！你沒看見牆上"禁止吸煙"的標誌嗎？

字 彙

feel 感覺	hot 熱；燙
open 打開	window 窗戶
smoke 抽菸	certainly 當然；無疑地
sign 標誌	wall 牆壁

18. Do you drink?

你喝酒嗎？

說 明

　　當你自己是個喜歡喝酒或是會喝酒的人，而想問對方是否也是如此時，或是想邀請對方喝酒，就可以問他這句話。或者，你只是想知道對方是否會喝酒，也可以用此句表達。雖然 drink 有喝東西的意思，例如：drink water(喝水)、drink milk(喝牛奶)，但用在此情況下，就是指喝酒，且後面不加 wine(酒)。

情境對話 1：

Ⓐ Do you drink, David?
大衛，你喝酒嗎？

Ⓑ No, I don't drink.
不，我不喝酒的。

情境對話 2：

Ⓐ The white wine tastes good. But, do you drink?
這白酒嚐起來不錯。但是你喝酒嗎？

Ⓑ Yes, sometimes I drink。
我有時候會小酌一番。

字　彙

drink 喝	white 白色
wine 酒	taste 品嚐
sometimes 有時候	

19. Does it work?

那有用嗎？

說　明

當對方想用他自己的方式來解決或處理一件事情時，而你懷疑他的方法是否有效時，就可以這麼跟他說 Does it work？若強調語氣，就可以說 Does it really work？

情境對話 1：

Ⓐ I want to let Henry deal with this program.
我想讓亨利處理這項計畫。

Ⓑ Does it work? I don't think he can do it well.
那有用嗎？我不相信他會做得好。

情境對話2：

Ⓐ Does it work? Won't you worry about the consequence if you do so?

那有用嗎？你不擔心你這麼做的後果嗎？

Ⓑ I will take the responsibility.

我會負責的。

字　彙

worry 擔心　　　　　　　　consequence 後果、結果

responsibility 責任

20. Don't you know?

你不知道嗎？

說　明

當你認為某件事情是大家都知道，但卻有人不清楚或未聽聞該事時，就可以跟對方說這句話來表示你的驚訝。

情境對話1：

Ⓐ What? Sarah got married!

什麼？莎拉結婚了！

Ⓑ Don't you know? It has been a while.

你不知道嗎？她結婚已經有一段時間了耶。

情境對話2：

Ⓐ Don't you know you'll be fined if you dump here?

你不知道在這倒垃圾會被罰款嗎？

Ⓑ No, I didn't know. Thanks for telling me.

不，我不知道。謝謝你告訴我。

字 彙

married 結婚的	while 一會兒、一段時間
fine 罰款	dump 傾倒；倒垃圾

21. Feel better?

有好點嗎？

說 明

當對方身體或心理受傷時，且恢復完一陣時間後，就可以用這句話來表達你對對方的關心，屬於慰問的語氣。

情境對話1：

Ⓐ Feel better?
有好點嗎？

Ⓑ Yes, after taking a rest I feel better now. Thanks!
有，休息過後我覺得有好點了。謝謝！

情境對話2：

Ⓐ Do you feel better after breaking up with James?
和詹姆士分手後有好點嗎？

Ⓑ No. I still feel pain.
不，我還是覺得很痛苦。

字 彙

rest 休息	after 在~之後
break up 分手	pain 痛苦

22. Guess what?

猜猜看？

說　明

　　當你要敘述一件會令人感到驚訝的事情時，則可以用這句話在句首上。另外，Guess what？從字面上來看是猜猜看發生了什麼事的意思，但實際上人家絕不是要你去猜發生了什麼事，而只是想要給對方一個驚喜，就如同中文"你知道嗎？"是一樣的。

情境對話1：

Ⓐ Guess what?
　　猜猜看？

Ⓑ What?
　　什麼事？

Ⓐ Judy is pregnant!
　　茱蒂懷孕了！

情境對話2：

Ⓐ Guess what happened to the project?
　　猜猜看這項方案如何？

Ⓑ It passed?
　　它通過了？

字　彙

pregnant 懷孕的　　　　　　happen 發生
passed (pass 的過去式) 通過

23. How about that?

你覺得那個如何呢？

說　明

　當你想問對方關於某個你有興趣的事物的看法時，就可以用這句話問他。

情境對話1：

Ⓐ I like purple skirts. Unh, how about that?
我喜歡紫色的裙子。呃，你覺得那件如何呢？

Ⓑ Not bad! It suits you.
還不錯啊！它很適合你。

情境對話2：

Ⓐ How about that? The green teapot.
你覺得那個如何呢？那個綠色的茶壺。

Ⓑ I prefer the brown one.
我比較喜歡咖啡色的。

字　彙

purple 紫色	skirt 裙子
suit 適合	green 綠色
teapot 茶壺	prefer 偏好
brown 咖啡色、棕色	

24. How can you say that?

你怎麼可以這樣說？

說　明

　當你聽見對方或有人對於某件事情或某個人的評論過於粗魯、沒禮貌亦或偏激時，有造成傷害之虞時，就可以跟他說這句話來表示你的不同意或不滿。也可以說成 How can you say so？

情境對話 1：

Ⓐ I will never see him again!
我再也不要見到他！

Ⓑ How can you say that? He is your dad after all.
你怎麼可以這樣說？他終究是你爸。

情境對話 2：

Ⓐ How can you say that? It's not all my fault!
你怎麼可以這樣說？這又不全然是我的錯！

Ⓑ Then, please explain it.
那麼，請你解釋一下。

字　彙

never 絕不	again 再一次
after all 終究	fault 過錯
then 那麼；當時	explain 解釋

25. How come?

為什麼？

說　明

此句等同於 Why？但含有責備或質詢的語氣，較少用在正式的場合中。

情境對話 1：

Ⓐ I don't want to go to school today.
我今天不想去上學。

Ⓑ How come?
為什麼？

Ⓐ I don't feel well.
我身體不舒服。

情境對話2：

Ⓐ I failed the exam.
我這次考試不及格。

Ⓑ How come? You studied hard during that period of time !
為什麼？你那段時間很用功讀書啊！

字　彙

school 學校	today 今天
study hard 用功讀書	during 在~期間
period 期間、時期	

26. How could you do this to me?

你怎麼可以這樣對我呢？

說　明

當你發現對方對你做了不該做的事情或傷害你時，就可以用上此句以表達不滿或憤怒，有時甚至帶有遺憾的意味。通常用在你認識的熟人、親友或同事之間的對話。

情境對話1：

Ⓐ How could you do this to me?
你怎麼可以這樣對我呢？

Ⓑ I didn't mean it.
我不是故意的。

情境對話2：

Ⓐ How could you do this to me?
你怎麼可以這樣對我呢？

Ⓑ You cheated on me first!
是你先欺騙我的！

字　彙

mean 意指；意圖　　　　　cheated (cheat 的過去式) 欺騙
first 最初；首先

27. How do you feel?

你感覺如何？

說　明

　　當你想詢問對方身體或心理狀態有無改善時，就可以用此句表達。另外，此句也可以用在詢問對方關於你自己所設定或已有先入為主看法、意見的事物，以徵求或參考對方的意見。通常會接about+所詢問的東西(名詞)，例如，**How do you feel about the book**？

情境對話1：

Ⓐ How do you feel after taking medicine?
服完藥後你感覺如何？

Ⓑ I feel great now!
我現在覺得好極了！

情境對話2：

Ⓐ How do you feel about Internet dating?
你覺得網路交友如何呢？

Ⓑ Well, I think you should be careful of some invisible traps.
我想你應該要小心提防某些看不見的陷阱。

字　彙

medicine 藥　　　　　　　the Internet 網路
dating 約會；交友　　　　　think 想；認為
should 應該　　　　　　　careful 小心的
invisible 隱形的；隱藏的　　trap 陷阱

28. How long does it take?

那要花多久的時間？

說　明

當你想知道某事物會花多少時間來處理或等待時，就可以用這句話來問對方。且這裡 "花時間" 的 "花" 一定要用 take。

情境對話1：

Ⓐ How long does it take?
那要多久的時間？

Ⓑ I'm not sure. Maybe twenty minutes.
我不確定。也許要二十分鐘。

情境對話2：

Ⓐ How long does it take from here to the train station?
從這裡到火車站要花多久的時間？

Ⓑ It takes about fifteen minutes.
大約十五分鐘。

字　彙

twenty 二十	from 從
train station 火車站	take 花費(時間)
fifteen 十五	

29. How much?

多少錢？

說　明

當你想詢問某物的價錢時，就可以用此句。也可以說 How much does it cost？而這裡的 "花多少錢" 的 "花" 則要用 cost。或者用 How much is it？也可以。

情境對話1：

Ⓐ How much is the bill?
這帳單多少錢？

Ⓑ It is seven hundred dollars.
七百元。

情境對話2：

Ⓐ How much does this pair of jeans cost?
這條牛仔褲多少錢？

Ⓑ It costs two thousand dollars.
兩千元。

字 彙

bill 帳單　　　　　　　　hundred 百
pair 對；雙　　　　　　　jeans 牛仔褲
cost 花費(金錢)

30. How've you been lately?

最近過得如何？

說 明

　當你久未與友人聯絡，或想知道他的近況時，即可用此句以表達你的關心或慰問之意。lately 也可以改成 recently，且與現在完成式(have+Vp.p.)並用。

情境對話1：

Ⓐ How've you been lately, Wesley?
衛斯理，最近過得如何？

Ⓑ Not so bad. But I just moved to another place.
還不錯。但我搬到另外一個地方去了。

情境對話2：

Ⓐ I haven't seen you for so long, Timmy. How've you been lately?

提米，很久沒見到你了。最近過的如何？

Ⓑ Well, as usual. Nothing changes.

就如同往常。沒什麼改變。

字 彙

lately 最近	move 搬家；移動
another 另一(個)	place 地方
usual 通常、平常的	change 改變

31. How's it going?

一切都還好嗎？

說 明

當你想跟對方打招呼時，即使是沒有很熟的朋友，也可以說 How's it going？另外，若只是單純想知道對方所做的活動或事情進行的情況，或是對方個人的近況如何時，也可以用這句話來問對方，以示關心。

情境對話1：

Ⓐ Hey, Dave. How's it going?

嘿，戴夫。一切都還好嗎？

Ⓑ Good. Everything goes smoothly.

很好。一切都很順利。

情境對話2：

Ⓐ How's it going with the meeting?

會議一切都還順利嗎？

B Well, it went through as scheduled.

嗯，就如計畫進行。

字　彙

smoothly　順利地　　　　　　go through　進行；經過

schedule　行程表；計畫表

32. Is it true or false?

這是對的還是錯的？

說　明

當你想知道某事的資訊或某問題的答案是對還是錯時，就可以用這句話來表示你的疑惑。

情境對話1：

A Is it true or false?

這是對的還是錯的？

B Of course it's true!

當然是對的！

情境對話2：

A Is it true or false about the gossip?

關於這個八卦消息是對的還是錯的？

B I'm not sure about it, either.

我也不確定。

字　彙

gossip　八卦消息

33. Is that clear?

這樣清楚嗎？

說　明

當你想確定聆聽者是否聽懂你所表達的意思時，就可以用這句話詢問對方。

情境對話 1：

Ⓐ Is that clear, everyone?
各位，這樣清楚嗎？

Ⓑ Yes.
是的，清楚。

情境對話 2：

Ⓐ Is that clear about what I just said, Eric?
艾瑞克，關於我剛所說的，你這樣清楚嗎？

Ⓑ Pardon me. I'm still not quite clear about what you said.
不好意思，你可以再說一次嗎？我還是不太清楚你剛所說的。

字　彙

clear 清楚的；清澈的	just 剛剛；只是
pardon 原諒；寬恕	quite 相當

34. Is that so?

是這樣嗎？

說　明

當你對於對方所說的話或意見有疑問時，或是不太同意對方所說的話或是觀念時，就可以用此句表達。另外，同理也可用在對某件事情或報章雜誌新聞有不同看法的情況時。

情境對話1：

Ⓐ I think Jeffery is the smartest student at this school.
我認為傑佛瑞是學校裡最聰明的學生。

Ⓑ Is that so?
是這樣嗎？

情境對話2：

Ⓐ Is that so? Dad will come back from Spain this weekend?
是這樣嗎？爸這週末會從西班牙回來？

Ⓑ Yes, I'm sure. He told me in the mail.
是的，我確定。他在信裡告訴我的。

字　彙

smartest 最聰明的　　　　student 學生
Spain 西班牙　　　　　　weekend 週末
told(tell 的過去式)告訴　mail 信件

35. Is that yours?

那是你的嗎？

說　明

　當你看見某件物品在桌上或任意一個位置時，附近也有人時，就可以用這句話問他東西是不是你的。

情境對話1：

Ⓐ Is that yours?
那是你的嗎？

Ⓑ No, it's not mine.
不，那不是我的。

情境對話2：

Ⓐ Grey, is that yours?
格雷，那是你的嗎？

Ⓑ Yes! I have been looking for my cell phone for three days. Thank you!
是的！我找我的手機找了三天了。

字　彙

mine 我的　　　　　　　　look for 尋找
cell phone 手機

36. Is there anything wrong?

有什麼問題嗎？

說　明

當你敘述完一件事情，或操作、示範完某個儀器或動作後，發現對方的表情似乎有些疑惑時，就可以問他 Is there anything wrong?如果對方還是有問題，就再跟他解釋。此句後面若要加名詞，介系詞要用 with。例如：Is there anything wrong with the picture? (關於這張圖有什麼問題嗎？)

情境對話1：

Ⓐ Is there anything wrong with the sentence?
這句子有什麼問題嗎？

Ⓑ It's missing a conjunction.
它少了一個連接詞。

情境對話2：

Ⓐ Is there anything wrong with the machine?
這台機器有什麼問題嗎？

Ⓑ Yes, it's out of function.
有，它故障了。

字 彙

sentence 句子　　　　　　　miss 漏掉；錯失
conjunction 連接詞　　　　　machine 機器
out of function 故障

37. May I? 019

我可以嗎？

說 明

　當別人邀請你參與某個活動，例如：Do you want to come to the par-ty?(你想來參加這次的派對嗎？)你就可以回說 May I?(我可以嗎？)。或是，當你想做某件事情，也可以用這句話來尋求他人的同意。例如：May I open the window?(我可以打開窗戶嗎？)此句為較有禮貌、謙虛的表達方式。通常若要加所做的事情，後面則要加原形動詞。

情境對話1：

Ⓐ I hope you can take the trip with us.
我希望你能跟我們一起去旅遊。

Ⓑ May I?
我可以嗎？

情境對話2：

Ⓐ May I go to the restroom?
我可以上廁所嗎？

Ⓑ Yes, you may.
當然可以。

字 彙

trip 旅行　　　　　　　　　restroom 廁所

38. May I ask some questions?

我可以問幾個問題嗎？

說　明

當你對於老師或對方所説的事情不懂時，就可以用這句話問對方。句尾再加 please 會更顯禮貌性，但不加也可。

情境對話1：

Ⓐ May I ask some questions?
我可以問幾個問題嗎？

Ⓑ Sure, go ahead.
當然可以，隨你問。

情境對話2：

Ⓐ Sir, may I ask some questions about this article?
老師，我可以問幾個有關這篇文章的問題嗎？

Ⓑ Yes. What are they?
可以。是哪些問題呢？

字　彙

question 問題　　　　　go ahead 請便
article 文章

39. May I help you?

我可以幫你嗎？

說　明

當你看見或發現有人需要幫忙時，就可以用上此句。也可以説 Can I help you?但用 may 較為禮貌，對方也會感覺有受到尊重的感覺。

情境對話1：

Ⓐ May I help you?
我可以幫你嗎？

Ⓑ No, thanks. I can do it myself.
不，謝了。我可以自己來。

情境對話2：

Ⓐ May I help you, madam?
夫人，我可以幫你嗎？

Ⓑ Oh, yes. Can you help me find my glasses?
喔，好啊！你可以幫我找我的眼鏡嗎？

字　彙

myself 我自己　　　　　madam (對婦女的恭敬稱呼)
　　　　　　　　　　　　夫人、太太、小姐

glasses 眼鏡

40. Really?

真的嗎？

說　明

當對方所說的話讓你感到驚訝或懷疑時，就可以用這句話回應。

情境對話1：

Ⓐ I'm going to leave for Japan tomorrow.
我明天就要去日本了。

Ⓑ Really?
真的嗎？

Ⓐ I have arranged this trip for a month.
我安排這次旅程一個月了。

情境對話2：

Ⓐ Really? Did she really say that?
真的嗎？她真的那麼説？

Ⓑ Yes, she did!
是的，她真的這麼説了。

字　彙

Japan　日本　　　　　　　　arrange　安排

41. So what?

那又如何？

說　明

　　當你對某人所説的話或聽到某事情的結果，讓你感到不以為意時，就可以説 So what?此句含有不屑之意味，盡量少在正式場合中使用。

情境對話1：

Ⓐ I heard that Jessica won the champion in this speech contest.
我聽説潔西卡贏得這次演講比賽的冠軍。

Ⓑ So what?
那又如何？

情境對話2：

Ⓐ So what? I can do much better than Tom!
那又如何？我可以做得比湯姆還要更好！

Ⓑ Are you sure?
你確定嗎？

字　彙

won(win 的過去式)贏、勝利　　champion 冠軍

speech 演講　　　　　　　　much 大量；許多；遠為~得多

42. That can't be right, can it?

那不可能是對的，是嗎？

說　明

當你覺得某事的結果讓你覺得不可置信的糟糕，或結果是較為負面的情況時，就能用此句表達你的震驚或疑惑。

情境對話1：

Ⓐ That can't be right, can it?
那不可能是對的，是嗎？

Ⓑ It's hard to say.
這很難說。

情境對話2：

Ⓐ The bill of your cell phone number this month cost ten thousand dollars.
你這個月的手機帳單費用是一萬元。

Ⓑ That can't be right, can it? There must be something wrong with the bill!
那不可能是對的，是嗎？一定是帳單有出錯！

字　彙

hard 困難　　　　　　　　bill 帳單

number 號碼　　　　　　　ten thousand 萬

43. What are you doing?

你在做什麼？

說　明

　當你看見對方正從事某件你不知道或不清楚的事時，就可以用這句話問他。或者，也可以用這句話來質詢對方，使之瞭解現在是什麼樣的情況。例如，上課的時候，學生應該專心聽課，而非與他人聊天。

情境對話1：

Ⓐ What are you doing, Mark?
　馬克，你在做什麼？

Ⓑ I am fixing my bike.
　我在修理我的腳踏車。

情境對話2：

Ⓐ What are you doing? Don't you know it's class time?
　你在做什麼？你不知道現在是上課時間嗎？

Ⓑ I'm sorry.
　對不起。

字　彙

fix 修理　　　　　　　　　bike 腳踏車

class 課程；班級

44. What can I do for you?

我可以幫你什麼嗎？

說　明

　當你發覺有人需要幫忙時，你就可以用這句話。但通常此句多用在服務生與客人之間的對話。

情境對話1：

Ⓐ What can I do for you, sir?
先生，我可以幫你什麼嗎？

Ⓑ Please give me a cup of tea. Thanks!
請給我一杯茶，謝謝！

情境對話2：

Ⓐ What can I do for you, Miss Dora?
朵拉小姐，我可以幫你什麼嗎？

Ⓑ Nothing, thanks.
不用，謝謝。

字 彙

cup 杯子   tea 茶

45. What day is today?

今天星期幾？

說 明

當你不知道今天是星期幾時，就可以用這句話問對方。day 不同於 date，date 是指明確的日期，但是 day 則大多指星期。

情境對話1：

Ⓐ What day is today?
今天星期幾？

Ⓑ It's Thursday.
今天星期四。

情境對話2：

Ⓐ What day is today, Sally?
莎莉，今天星期幾？

B I don't know. Let me take a look at the calendar.
我不知道。我看一下日曆。

字 彙

Thursday 星期四　　　　　　calendar 日曆

---

46. **What did you say?**

你剛說什麼？

說 明

　　當你聽不清楚對方所說的話時，就可以用這句話問他。另外，當你覺得對方所說的話帶有挑釁的意味或讓你有不悅的感覺時，也可以用這句話來反問對方。例如：What did you say? You mean I am too rude? (你是說我太粗魯嗎？)

情境對話1：

A Excuse me. What did you say?
不好意思。你剛說什麼？

B I said let's celebrate Henry's birthday this Sunday.
我說我們這周日來慶祝亨利的生日吧！

情境對話2：

A What did you say? I can't hear you.
你剛說什麼？我聽不到你說的話。

B I said we should leave right now.
我說我們現在該走了。

字 彙

celebrate 慶祝　　　　　　birthday 生日
leave 離開

47. **What do you do?** (024)

你是做什麼工作？

說 明

如果你想知道對方的職業時，就可以用這句話。此句也等同於 What's your job?

情境對話1：

Ⓐ What do you do, Johnson?
強森，你是做什麼工作？

Ⓑ I am an accountant.
我做會計的。

情境對話2：

Ⓐ What do you do?
你是做什麼工作？

Ⓑ I am an engineer.
我是工程師。

字 彙

accountant 會計師　　　　　engineer 工程師

48. **What do you mean?**

你是指什麼意思？

說 明

此句話有兩種情況，一是你不了解對方所表達的意思時，就可以問他這句話。另一種則是，你知道對方所要表達的意思，但其意思讓你感覺很不是滋味或很生氣時，就能用此句來反詰之。

情境對話1：

Ⓐ What do you mean? I don't understand.
你是指什麼意思？我不懂。

Ⓑ I mean you can try another method to resolve the question.
我是指說你可以試看看用別的方式來解決這個問題。

情境對話2：

Ⓐ What do you mean? Am I not qualified enough to be your husband?
你是指什麼意思？難道我不夠格當你的丈夫嗎？

Ⓑ Yes, that's what I mean!
沒錯，正是此意！

字　彙

try 嘗試	method 方式
resolve 解決	qualified 有資格的
husband 丈夫	

49. What do you want? (025)

你想怎麼樣？

說　明

當你覺得對方對你有所意圖時，或者不滿對方所提出的條件時，就可以用這句話反問之。另外，對方可能無意間說出令你不悅的話，而你也恰巧聽見時，也可以用這句話反擊。通常此句的表達方式是不太有禮貌的，盡量少在正式場合用，不然會很容易與對方起爭執。跟 What do you mean? 的意思比起來，語氣多少還是有些差別。

情境對話1：

Ⓐ What do you want?
你想怎麼樣？

B Nothing. I didn't say anything.
沒事。我什麼都沒說。

情境對話2：

A What do you want?
你想怎麼樣？

B You owe me an apology. That's all!
你欠我一個道歉。就是這樣而已！

字 彙

anything 任何事	owe 欠
apology 道歉	

50. What does it do?

這個有甚麼用？

說 明

當你想知道某物品的用途為何時，或是懷疑某物品(藥物、保健食品、儀器等)是否真有其所說的效果時，就可以用這句話問對方。

情境對話1：

A What does it do?
這個有甚麼用？

B Here. You can read the instructions on the box.
這邊。你可以看一下箱子上的使用說明。

情境對話2：

A What does it do? Is it helpful for our health?
這個有甚麼用？它對我們的健康有幫助嗎？

B I can't guarantee it'll effect you, but most people believe it works.
我不能跟你保證它的效果，但是大部分的人都相信它有用。

字　彙

instructions 使用說明	helpful 有幫助的
health 健康	guarantee 保證
effect 效果	most 大部分的
believe 相信	

51. What does that mean? (026)

那是什麼意思？

說　明

當你看見或聽見某個讓你摸不著頭緒，或是不解其意的事情時，就可以用這句話來請教對方。

情境對話1：

Ⓐ What does that mean?
那是什麼意思？

Ⓑ It means that you need a key to open the box.
它是指說你需要一把鑰匙來打開這個盒子。

情境對話2：

Ⓐ What does that mean? The traffic sign looks unclear.
那是什麼意思？這個交通標誌看起來很不清楚。

Ⓑ It says, "No enter!"
它是指 "禁止進入！"

字　彙

traffic 交通	sign 標誌；號誌
unclear 不清楚的	enter 進入

52. What happened?

發生什麼事？

說　明

當你不了解某事情的情況或原由時，就可以用這句話詢問他人。此句通常是指已經發生過的事，所以 happen 要加 ed，以代表過去式。而 What is happening？通常則指目前正在發生的事，所以用現在進行式。

情境對話1：

🅐 What happened?
發生什麼事？

🅑 Hank got drunk again.
漢克又喝醉了。

情境對話2：

🅐 What happened to Kelly yesterday?
凱莉昨天發生什麼事？

🅑 Peter didn't see her coming and hit her by accident.
彼得沒有看見她走過來，而不小心打到她。

字　彙

drunk 喝醉的   hit 打
by accident 碰巧；意外

53. What have I done?

(027)

我做了什麼？

說　明

通常此句用在對自己所做的事感到懊悔或深感遺憾、悔恨時，就會對自己說 What have I done？

情境對話1：

Ⓐ Wells, do you know you ruined the wedding ceremony?
威爾斯，你知道你搞砸了這場婚禮了嗎？

Ⓑ Gosh! What have I done?
天哪！我做了什麼？

情境對話2：

Ⓐ What have I done? I almost lost my child.
我做了什麼？我差點失去了我的小孩。

Ⓑ You should stop gambling and drinking.
你應該戒賭和戒酒。

字　彙

ruined (ruin 的過去式) 破壞；搞砸

wedding ceremony 婚禮　　　gambling 賭博

drinking 喝酒

54. What's new?

有什麼新鮮事？

說　明

　此句常用於和熟識友人之間的問候或打招呼之語用，例如，當你與朋友碰面時，就可以問他 What's new？來開頭，順便問他最近是否有耳聞一些新的資訊或消息。

情境對話1：

Ⓐ Hey, Kay! What's new?
嘿，有什麼新鮮事？

Ⓑ Mnn. Nothing special.
嗯，沒什麼特別的。

情境對話2：

Ⓐ What's new today?
今天有什麼新鮮事嗎？

Ⓑ Rumor has it that the manager will soon resign.
據傳聞經理不久就要辭職。

字　彙

special 特別的	rumor 謠言、謠傳
manager 經理	soon 很快；不久
resign 辭職	

55. What's the meaning of this?　(028)

這是什麼意思？

說　明

這句話有兩種含意。一是純粹用以詢問某件事物的含意；另一種則是當對方說出讓你感到生氣或不滿的話時，就可以回他這句話。另外，this 可以換成任何你想詢問的名詞，例如：What's the meaning of life？(生命的意義究竟為何？)

情境對話1：

Ⓐ What's the meaning of this? Could you explain it?
這是什麼意思？可以請你解釋一下嗎？

Ⓑ Ok! But it may take an hour.
可以啊！但可能要花上一個小時來解釋。

情境對話2：

Ⓐ Someone said you're not suitable for this position.
有人說你不適合這職位。

Ⓑ What's the meaning of this? Who said so?
這是什麼意思？是誰這麼說的？

字　彙

suitable 適合的

position 職位

56. What's up?

有什麼事嗎？

說　明

　此句最常用來打招呼，特別是熟人之間見面時的問候。或者，的確是問對方真有什麼事情的意思。

情境對話1：

Ⓐ What's up?
有什麼事嗎？

Ⓑ Nothing. Same as always.
沒事。就和平常一樣。

情境對話2：

Ⓐ What's up? Bill.
比爾，有什麼事嗎？

Ⓑ I just got an interview at a high-tech company.
我最近得到一個高科技公司的面試機會。

Ⓐ Wow! That sounds great!
哇！聽起來很不錯！

字　彙

same 一樣	always 總是
interview 面試	high-tech 高科技

57. What's wrong?

(029)

怎麼了？

說　明

　　當你聽見某個讓你驚訝或疑惑的消息，又或者是看見某人似乎處於負面情緒狀態時(如：悲傷、生氣等)，就可以問對方這句話，以示關心、了解事情的原由。有時後面會加上 with you，但意思有時可能帶有責問對方的語氣，就會變成是"你是怎麼回事啊？"的意思。

情境對話1：

🅐 What's wrong? Dear. Why are you crying?
親愛的，怎麼了？你為什麼哭？

🅑 Mom, they all say I am a freak.
媽，他們都說我是怪胎。

情境對話2：

🅐 What's wrong with the place? It's a mess!
這地方是怎麼了？真是一團亂！

🅑 You are not the first one to say so.
你不是第一個這麼說的人。

字　彙

dear 親愛的

all 都；全部

freak 怪胎；怪異的

mess 一團亂

58. What's your problem?

你是怎麼回事啊？

說　明

　若你的朋友、家人、同事或員工做了一件讓你很生氣又震撼的事時，或聽到他們這麼做時，就可以當著他們的面說這句話。但此句的語氣有些過重，甚至是有指責的語氣，所以通常是用於認識一段時間以上的人身上。

情境對話1：

Ⓐ What's your problem? You think everyone is just like you?
你是怎麼回事啊？你以為每個人都像你一樣啊？

Ⓑ No, I don't think like that.
不，我沒有這麼想。

情境對話2：

Ⓐ I screwed up the plan, but I didn't mean it.
我搞砸了這個計畫，但我不是故意的。

Ⓑ What's your problem? Why did you do that?
你是怎麼回事啊？你為什麼這麼做？

字　彙

like 像；喜歡

screw up 搞砸

problem 問題

59. **What should I do?**

（030）

> 我該怎麼辦？

說　明

　　此句可用於兩種情況，一是當你碰到不知該如何解決一項難題時，就可以用這句話來尋求他人的協助或建議。另一種則是，當你遇上某些事而使心理受到挫折或打擊時，例如：分手、失去家人或意外事故等，就會跟自己對話說 What should I do？以示內心的無助與脆弱。

情境對話1：

A What should I do? I don't know how to operate this machine.

我該怎麼辦？我不知道怎麼操作這台機器。

B It's ok. Let me show you.

沒關係。我示範一次給你看。

情境對話2：

A I lost my job and broke up with Helen. What should I do?

我丟了工作又和海倫分手。我該怎麼辦？

B Well, just let them go.

唉，就讓他們去吧！

字　彙

operate 操作

show 展現

lost(lose 的過去式)失去；遺失

60. What were you thinking?

你在想什麼啊?

說 明

當你聽見你的親友說了或犯了一些蠢事或錯誤時,就可以用此句話來責問他。

情境對話1:

A Ray, I broke dad's favorite vase by accident.
雷,我不小心打破了爸最心愛的花瓶。

B What were you thinking? It cost fifty thousand dollars!
你在想什麼啊?那支花瓶價值五十萬!

情境對話2:

A What were you thinking? You shouldn't have done that! It's illegal!
你在想什麼啊?你不該這麼做的!那是違法的!

B But no one saw it.
但是又沒人看見。

字 彙

broke(break 的過去式)破壞   vase 花瓶

illegal 違法的   saw(see 的過去式)看見

61. What would you like?   031

你想要什麼?

說 明

此句後面通常會再加動詞,例如 What would you like to be?(你想要當什麼?)、What would you like to change?(你想要改變什麼?)

情境對話1：

Ⓐ What would you like to eat for dinner?
你晚餐想要吃什麼？

Ⓑ I would like a hamburger and cola.
我想吃漢堡和可樂。

情境對話2：

Ⓐ What would you like to be when you grow up, Justin?
賈斯汀，你長大後想做什麼？

Ⓑ I would like to fly an airplane.
我想要開飛機。

字　彙

dinner 晚餐	hamburger 漢堡
cola 可樂	grow 成長
airplane 飛機	

62. What would you say?

你覺得怎樣？

說　明

當你想詢問對方關於你的想法或選擇有何看法時，就可以用上這句話。

情境對話1：

Ⓐ What would you say about this idea?
你覺得這個主意怎樣？

Ⓑ It sounds good!
聽起來不錯啊！

情境對話2：

Ⓐ Pam, what would you say if I change my present job?
潘，你覺得如果我換掉目前的工作怎樣？

Ⓑ You can give it a try if you want.
如果你想的話就試看看囉！

字　彙

idea 主意　　　　　　　　　　present 現在的

---

63. Who do you think you are?

你以為你是誰？

說　明

　當你覺得對方來意不善，或是有些自以為是時，或表現出瞧不起人的意味時，就可以用這句話。但是這句話少用於正式場合中，因為此句的語氣有些過重，易引起不必要的爭執。

情境對話1：

Ⓐ You came to my home without permission and yelled at my family. Who do you think you are?
你未經允許擅自到我家又對我的家人大吼。你以為你是誰？

Ⓑ Sorry, I was drunk that time.
對不起，我當時喝醉了。

情境對話2：

Ⓐ Who do you think you are? I'm not your babysitter!
你以為你是誰？我又不是你的保姆！

Ⓑ Fine! I could do it myself!
好啊！我就自己來！

字 彙

without 沒有	permission 允許
yell 吼叫	babysitter 保姆

64. Who do you think you are talking to?

你以為你在跟誰說話？

說 明

當有人用很不客氣的口氣跟你說話時，就可以用這句話來回應以表示你的不滿。

情境對話1：

Ⓐ Who do you think you are talking to? I'm in charge of this company!
你以為你在跟誰說話？我才是這間公司的老闆！

Ⓑ Sorry! I didn't know that.
抱歉！我不知道你是老闆。

情境對話2：

Ⓐ Hey! Go get my coffee.
嘿！把我的咖啡拿來。

Ⓑ Wait! Who do you think you are talking to?
等一下！你以為你在跟誰說話？

字 彙

in charge of 負責人

coffee 咖啡

65. Who's calling?

（033）

是哪一位？

說　明

　當你接起電話要問是誰打來時，就可以用這句話問對方，而不是問 Who are you？因為在電話中並未親眼見到對方，所以要說 Who's calling？(who's=who is)

情境對話1：

A Hello! Is Nancy there?
哈囉！南西在嗎？

B Yes, she's in. Who's calling, please?
是的，她在。請問哪一位？

情境對話2：

A Who's calling?
是哪一位？

B It's me, Barry.
是我，貝瑞。

字　彙

there 在那裡　　　　　　　　　call 打電話；喊叫

66. Who knows?

誰知道？

說　明

　當有人問你不知道的事情，或是你不知該如何回答的問題時，除了回說 I don't know.(我不知道。)外，也可以說 Who knows？

情境對話1：

Ⓐ Why does Kate want to marry Albert?
為什麼凱特想嫁給艾伯特？

Ⓑ Who knows?
誰知道？

情境對話2：

Ⓐ How could a man do such a stupid thing?
怎麼會有人做這麼愚蠢的事呢？

Ⓑ Who knows?
誰知道？

字　彙

such 這樣的　　　　　　　　stupid 愚蠢的

---

67. Who says?　　（034）

誰說的？

說　明

當你聽見一件讓你很不以為意或是讓你感到驚訝的消息時，就可以用這句話來回應對方。

通常後面可再加一個完整的句子。

情境對話1：

Ⓐ Who says you can't go back?
誰說你不能回去？

Ⓑ It's Webber. He said I had to finish the work first.
是韋伯。他說我得先把工作完成。

情境對話2：

Ⓐ Generally, men will soon pass away after their wives die.
一般而言，男人在他們的妻子去世後，不久也會隨之而去。

Ⓑ Who says?
誰說的？

字　彙

generally 一般地	pass away 過世
die 死亡	wives (wife 的複數) 妻子

68. Who told you that?

誰告訴你的？

說　明

當你的友人跟你說了一件事情或消息，而你欲知對方是如何得知此事時，就可以問他這句話。此句話所要表達的含意有點類似 Who says？但這兩句的差異性在於 Who told you that？比較強調在 "到底是誰告訴你這件事" 的意味，詢問者是真的想知道 "消息傳播的來源"。

情境對話1：

Ⓐ Damn it! We can't get the budget of this project.
可惡！我們拿不到這項方案的預算。

Ⓑ Who told you that?
誰告訴你的？

情境對話2：

Ⓐ Grandma, am I an orphan?
奶奶，我是孤兒嗎？

Ⓑ Who told you that? It's nonsense!
誰告訴你的？胡說！

字　彙

damn 可惡	budget 預算
grandma 祖母	orphan 孤兒
nonsense 胡說	

69. Whose turn?　(035)

輪到誰？

說　明

　　當在進行一項活動或遊戲時，不知道輪到誰時，就可以拋出此句話來問大家。

情境對話1：

Ⓐ Whose turn?
輪到誰？

Ⓑ Oh, sorry! It's my turn.
喔，不好意思！是輪到我了。

情境對話2：

Ⓐ Whose turn to sweep the floor today?
今天輪到誰掃地？

Ⓑ It's Lucy's.
是露西。

字　彙

sweep 掃地

floor 地板

70. Which would you prefer?

你喜歡哪一個?

說　明

　當你和友人逛街買東西時,就可以問他 Which would you prefer? 你喜歡哪一個?而 which 後面可加一個所要選擇的東西,例如:which kind(哪一種)、 which color(哪種顏色)等。另外,服務生也會問你這句話來請你表明所要點的選項。

情境對話1:

Ⓐ Which flavor would you prefer? Strawberry or vanilla?
你喜歡哪一種口味?草莓還是香草?

Ⓑ Strawberry, please.
我要草莓。

情境對話2:

Ⓐ Which would you prefer? Pink or purple?
你喜歡哪一個?粉紅色還是紫色?

Ⓑ Uhm, I prefer purple.
嗯,我比較喜歡紫色。

字　彙

flavor 口味

strawberry 草莓

vanilla 香草

pink 粉紅色

71. Why not?

為什麼不呢？/有何不可？

說　明

此句話有兩種含意，一種是可以跟 Why？通用，同樣表達為什麼，想知道其原因的意思。另一種則是用一個較有禮貌或間接的方式 Why not？來對對方所提出的條件、請求或邀請以示"同意"或"接受"的意思，也可說是"有何不可"。

情境對話1：

Ⓐ I can't go shopping with you.
我不能跟你一起去購物了。

Ⓑ Why not?
為什麼不呢？

情境對話2：

Ⓐ If you don't mind I'll open the window.
如果你不介意的話，我要把窗戶打開了喔！

Ⓑ Why not?
有何不可？

字　彙

go shopping 採購

Chapter · **2**

一般對話常用答句

72. A one-way ticket, please. (036)

請給我一張單程票。

說 明

　不論是搭火車、船或飛機等交通工具，若只要一張去或是回的單程票時，就可以跟售票員說這句話。

情境對話1：

Ⓐ A one-way ticket, please.
請給我一張單程票。

Ⓑ To which place, sir?
先生，是到哪一個地方呢？

情境對話2：

Ⓐ A one-way ticket to Taipei, please.
請給我一張到台北的單程票。

Ⓑ Ok. Here you are.
好的。這是你要的票。

字 彙

one-way 單向的　　　　　　　ticket 票
sir 先生(對男性的尊稱)

73. After you!

你先請！

說 明

　當你要對對方表達禮貌或禮讓之意時，要請人家先走或請人家先做某件事情時，就可以用這句話表示。例如，在進出門或上車時的場合。

情境對話1：

A After you, Miss Mandy.
曼蒂小姐，你妳請。

B Thank you, Mr. Frank.
謝謝，法蘭克先生。

情境對話2：

A After you! I'll come later.
你先走！我待會就來。

B Ok.
好。

字　彙

later 稍後；待會

74. All right!　　(037)

好吧！/好的。/很好，沒事。

說　明

　　此句話有許多含意，因此要視上下文的意思來決定所要表達的意思為何，但大多脫離不了"好吧！/好的。/很好，沒事"這三種意思。但也有 All right？(好嗎？)這意思。

情境對話1：

A All right! I accept your invitation.
好吧！我接受你的邀請。

B That's great! Thanks a lot!
太好了！真是太感激了！

情境對話2：

A Sloan, remember to give me a call when you reach Germany.

史隆，到德國時記得打通電話回來。

B All right, mom.

好的，媽。

字　彙

accept 接受	invitation 邀請
reach 抵達	Germany 德國

75. Any day will do.

哪一天都行。

說　明

當對方問你何時或哪一天有空時，如果你的時間都允許的話，就可以用這句話回應對方。

情境對話1：

A When do you have free time to go fishing?

你哪天有空可以釣魚？

B Any day will do.

哪一天都行。

情境對話2：

A What day can you come to our company for an interview?

你哪一天可以到我們公司來面試呢？

B Any day will do.

哪一天都行。

字　彙

free time　空閒時

---

76. As above.

如前述所言/同上。

說　明

當所陳述的事情或規則，之前已經講過或寫過，而不想再重複時，就可以用這句簡短的語句表示。

情境對話1：

Ⓐ As above, I have explained these rules. So, do you have any questions?

如前述所言，我已經解釋過這些規則了。那麼你們還有其他問題嗎？

Ⓑ No.

沒有。

情境對話2：

Ⓐ Same as above. There's something wrong with the case.

如同前述所言一樣。這件事有問題。

Ⓑ Then, what should we do?

那麼，我們該怎麼做呢？

字　彙

rule　規則；條例

case　事情；案件

77. ASAP(= As soon as possible)

儘快

說　明

當你希望對方能盡快處理你的事情時，就可以跟他說這句話。

情境對話1：

Ⓑ When should I give you the report?
我應該何時給你這份報告呢？

Ⓑ ASAP.
儘快。

情境對話2：

Ⓐ Peter, send this parcel to Tyler ASAP. It's urgent!
彼得，儘快把這個包裹寄給泰勒。情況緊急！

Ⓑ Ok, I'll do it right now.
好的，我現在就去。

字　彙

send 寄送　　　　　　　　parcel 包裹
urgent 緊急的

78. Be careful!

(039)

小心！

說　明

當你希望對方注意自身安全時，就可以用這句話提醒他。

情境對話1：

Ⓐ Hunt, be careful when you drive the car.
杭特，開車時要小心。

Ⓑ I know.
我知道。

情境對話2：

Ⓐ Be careful if you would like to go abroad alone.
如果你想自己單獨出國的話，要注意自身安全。

Ⓑ Thank you for reminding me this.
謝謝你提醒我。

字　彙

go abroad 出國　　　　　　　alone 單獨

remind 提醒

79. Be my guest.

我請你。

說　明

當你想邀請對方吃一頓時，就可以說這句話。

情境對話1：

Ⓐ Let's go to Truffle for lunch!
我們午餐去吃那間松露餐廳吧！

Ⓑ But, it's very expensive.
可是那間餐廳很貴。

Ⓐ It's ok. Be my guest.
沒關係。我請你。

情境對話2：

Ⓐ Gina, be my guest! Come to my place to have dinner tonight.
吉娜，我請你！今晚到我家吃晚餐吧！

B Really? Thank you!
真的嗎？謝謝你！

字　彙

truffle 松露　　　　　　　expensive 昂貴的

---

80. Be quiet.

安靜。

說　明

　　此句常用於學校的場合，例如，學生過於吵鬧時，老師就會說 Be quiet.但也可用在工作場所或家中，或任何你希望當下的氣氛是安靜沒有吵雜聲時，就可以說 Be quiet.

情境對話1：

A Please be quiet, everyone. I have something important to tell you.
各位請安靜。我有重要的事要跟你們說。

情境對話2：

A Be quiet, you two! I can't hear what the teacher is saying.
你們兩個安靜！我聽不到老師說的話。

B Sorry.
對不起。

字　彙

important 重要的　　　　　teacher 老師

81. Behave yourself.

檢點些吧！

說　明

當你看到有人的言行舉止有些超過，讓你覺得不太合時宜，就可以跟他說這句話。但是這樣的話語，通常會是由長輩口中聽到。不過同輩之間也可以，只是要注意分寸，也不要輕易對陌生人或不熟的人講這句話。

情境對話1：

Ⓐ Jim, behave yourself! Stop fooling around every day.
吉姆，檢點些吧！不要每天遊手好閒。

Ⓑ Yes, dad.
是的，爸。

情境對話2：

Ⓐ It's class time, Paul and Rick. Behave yourself, please.
保羅、瑞克，現在是上課時間。請檢點些。

Ⓑ Yes, Miss Claire.
知道了，克萊爾小姐。

字　彙

fool around 遊手好閒

82. Believe it or not!

信不信由你!

說　明

當你告知對方一項消息時，但對方卻不太相信時，就可以跟他說這句話。若對方相信你說的話，那麼這句話就只是當作一種告訴對方消息的開場白而已。

情境對話1：

Ⓐ You say Eli passed the test? It's impossible!
你說伊萊通過了測驗？那是不可能的！

Ⓑ Believe it or not! His name is on the bulletin board.
信不信由你! 他的名字在布告欄上。

情境對話2：

Ⓐ Hey, believe it or not! Cassie just got a promotion and became the sales manager!
嘿，你信不信!凱西剛升職成為業務經理！

Ⓑ Oh! I feel so happy for her!
喔！我真為她感到開心！

字　彙

impossible 不可能的	bulletin board 布告欄
promotion 提升；晉級	sales 業務；銷售

83. Bingo!

你猜對了！

說　明

　當你想要告訴對方一件事情的結果，但卻不想直接告知其結論時，而是要人家猜測，然後對方猜對時，就可以跟他說這句話。另外，Bingo 這詞其實是從 "賓果" 這遊戲延伸而來，但現在大多是指 "你答對了" 的意思。

情境對話1：

Ⓐ Hanson, guess who is our new president?
漢森，你猜誰是我們的新董事長？

Ⓑ Uhm, will it be Ron?
嗯，會是榮恩嗎？

Ⓐ Bingo!
你猜對了！

情境對話2：

Ⓐ Bingo! But how do you know the result?
你猜對了！但你怎麼知道這結果？

Ⓑ Well, I just know it!
呃，我就是知道啊！

字　彙

guess 猜　　　　　　　　　president 董事長；總統
result 結果

---

84. **Bottoms up!**

乾杯！

說　明

這句話常用在希望大家一起喝酒或以酒示致意的宴會或聚餐的場合。但此句是指真的喝酒喝到該酒杯見底，與 cheers 一般的乾杯不同。

情境對話1：

Ⓐ Let's salute the new chief!
我們來向新主任致意吧！

Ⓑ Bottoms up!
乾杯！

情境對話2：

Ⓐ Bottoms up, everyone!
大家乾杯吧！

Ⓑ Cheers!
乾杯！

字 彙

salute 向~致敬   chief 主任；長官

85. Call me.

打給我。

說 明

當有人找你時(無論是否是以透過電話的方式)，但你卻忙碌時，就可以跟對方講這句話，請他待會再回電。又或者是你覺得對方需要幫忙時，也可以告訴他，請他打電話給你。

情境對話1：

Ⓐ Sorry, I'm busy now. Call me later.
不好意思，我正在忙。待會再打給我。

Ⓑ Ok, I see.
好，我知道了。

情境對話2：

Ⓐ Call me anytime if you need me, ok?
如果你需要我的話隨時可以打給我，好嗎？

Ⓑ Ok, I really appreciate your kindness!
好的，我真的很感謝你的好意！

字 彙

appreciate 感謝；欣賞

kindness 仁慈：好意

86. Certainly!

(043)

當然！

說　明

當別人對於你說的事情存有疑問時，可是你卻很有把握自己的回答時，就可以說這句話。另外，當對方想請你幫忙或是有所請求時，你也可以用這句話回答以表示同意。其意思等同於 Of course!還有 Sure!

情境對話1：

Ⓐ May I use your motorcycle?
我可以借用你的摩托車嗎？

Ⓑ Certainly!
當然！

情境對話2：

Ⓐ Will they accomplish the assignment in time?
他們能及時完成所分派的任務嗎？

Ⓑ Certainly! I have faith in them.
當然！我對他們有信心。

字　彙

use 使用	motorcycle 摩托車
accomplish 完成	assignment 分派的任務
in time 及時	faith 信心；信念

87. Check it out!

去看一看吧！

說　明

當你和友人遇到讓你們覺得很好奇或奇怪的事情，而你想一探究竟時，就可以跟你的朋友說這句話。

情境對話1：

Ⓐ Look! What's that?
看！那是什麼？

Ⓑ I don't know. Let's check it out!
我不知道。我們去看一看吧！

情境對話2：

Ⓐ I remember that I switched off the light. But the light is on now.
我記得我有關燈。但是燈現在是亮的。

Ⓑ It's weird. Let's check it out!
真奇怪。我們去看一看吧！

字　彙

switch off 關掉　　　　　　　light 燈
weird 詭異的

88. Come on!

來吧！

說　明

這句話有很多中文解釋，例如：來吧！/少來了，別裝了！/拜託！/沒關係(安慰之意)/別害羞(鼓勵對方)……等等，須視說話的語調、情境或上下文來斷定 come on 在這裡的意思為何。

情境對話1：

Ⓐ I want to go out with you, but I have things uncompleted.
我想和你們出去，但是我還有事情未完成。

Ⓑ Come on! You can do it tomorrow!
來吧！你可以明天做啊！

情境對話2：

Ⓐ Come on! We have to stay up to get this tough task done!

來吧！我們必須熬夜將這棘手的工作處理完！

字　彙

uncompleted 未完成的	stay up 熬夜
tough 堅韌；費勁的	task 任務；苦差事

89. Control yourself!

克制一下!

說　明

當你希望對方克制一下自己的言行舉止或情緒時，就可以跟他說這句話。

情境對話1：

Ⓐ Jack, control yourself! Don't shout in public.

傑克，克制一下！不要在大庭廣眾下大叫。

Ⓑ Sorry! I didn't notice that.

對不起！我沒注意到。

情境對話2：

Ⓐ Control yourself. Don't go crazy!

克制一下。別發瘋啊！

Ⓑ Ok, but this joke is too fun!

好，但是這笑話太好笑了！

字　彙

public 公眾的	notice 注意
crazy 瘋的	joke 笑話

90. Count me in. (045)

算我一份。

說　明

當你聽到某件你有興趣的事情，或想加入的活動時，就可以跟對方說這句話。

情境對話1：

Ⓐ Does anyone want to go to the Shilin night market this Saturday night?

這週六晚上有人想去士林夜市嗎？

Ⓑ Yes, count me in!

有，算我一份！

情境對話2：

Ⓐ I have heard a piece of news about making money. Are you interested?

我聽到一個關於賺錢的消息。你有興趣嗎？

Ⓑ That sounds good. Count me in!

那聽起來不錯。算我一份！

字　彙

night market 夜市　　　　make money 賺錢

interested 感興趣的

91. Easy come, easy go.

來得容易，去得也快。

說　明

意思是說輕易獲得的事物(例如：金錢、好工作、愛情等)，就會一樣容易的失去。這個句子可用在人們遇上壞事時，為了表現出他們覺得無能為力或是他們不擔心(即使實際上可能擔心)時使用。

情境對話1：

Ⓐ Oh my goodness! You just lost one thousand dollars in that poker game.
我的天啊！你剛剛在撲克牌賭局中輸掉1000塊。

Ⓑ Yeah, easy come, easy go.
是啊，來得容易，去得也快。

情境對話2：

Ⓐ Judy left you? You two were meant for each other.
茱蒂離開你了？你們倆應該是天生一對。

Ⓑ Well, easy come, easy go.
唉，來得容易，去得也快。

字　彙

goodness 天哪；善良；好意　poker 撲克牌遊戲
meant(mean 的過去式)意指　each other 彼此

92. Excuse me.

對不起，你可以再說一次嗎？/借過。

說　明

此句話有很多意思，可應用於麻煩人家時，就可跟對方說 Excuse me 請對方原諒一下。也可用在聽不清楚人家說的話時，就說 Excuse me 請他再說一次。或是借過以及單純的對不起。

情境對話1：

Ⓐ Excuse me. Does this bus go to the Central Park?
對不起, 這公車開往中央公園嗎？

Ⓑ Yes, it does.
是的，沒錯。

情境對話2：

Ⓐ Excuse me. May I borrow your note?
對不起，我可以借你的筆記嗎？

Ⓑ Yes, you may.
好啊，可以。

字　彙

central 中央的；中心的　　　borrow 借

---

93. Face the music.

面對現實。

說　明

此句原意是來自法國當時囚犯要被處死時，他們就會放音樂給他聽，讓他冷靜下來。現在則引申為面對現實，接受處罰的意思。

情境對話1：

Ⓐ I failed three subjects in the mid-term examination. I'm afraid to tell my mom.
我期中考有三科不及格。我好怕告訴我媽。

Ⓑ No. You must go home and face the music.
不。你必須回家並面對現實。

情境對話2：

Ⓐ Leo was caught cheating during his test.
里歐在這次考試期間被抓到作弊。

Ⓑ Now, he has to face the music.
現在，他必須面對現實。

字 彙

subject 科目
mid-term 期中的
examination 考試
afraid 恐怕的；害怕的
cheat 作弊

94. Fasten your seat belt. 047

繫好你的安全帶。

說 明

搭乘汽車、飛機等交通工具時，就可以用這句話提醒有安全帶座位者，要繫好安全帶。

情境對話1：

Ⓐ Tom. Fasten your seat belt when you drive.
湯姆，開車時要繫好你的安全帶。

Ⓑ Ok, I will remember that.
好的，我會記住的。

情境對話2：

Ⓐ Kids, don't forget to fasten your seat belt when in a car.
孩子們，坐車時不要忘記繫好你們的安全帶。

Ⓑ Yes, Miss Dianne.
是的，黛安小姐。

字 彙

kid 小孩子

95. First come, first served.

先到先得。

說　明

從字面上解釋就是先到的客人，就先接受服務。但也有另一說法為捷足先登，先到者先贏。

情境對話1：

A The rule of this game is "First come, first served." Any questions?

這遊戲的規則就是"先到先得"。有任何問題嗎？

B No.

沒有。

情境對話2：

A Do you agree with the saying" First come, first served."?

你同意"先到先得"這句諺語嗎？

B Well, it depends.

視情況而定囉！

字　彙

saying 諺語；言論　　　　　depend 相信；依賴

96. Follow me.　　　(048)

跟我來。

說　明

當你希望有人跟著你一起做動作，或是照著你說的去執行一件事情或活動時，就可以跟對方說這句話。

情境對話1：

Ⓐ Follow me and you will know the truth of this matter.
跟我來你就會知道這件事情的真相。

Ⓑ Really?
真的嗎？

情境對話2：

Ⓐ Follow me and say "One, two! One, two!"
跟著我說 "一、二！一、二！"

Ⓑ "One, two! One, two!"
"一、二！一、二！"

字　彙

truth 事實；真相　　　　　matter 事情

---

97. Forget it.
算了。

說　明

當別人不小心對你做了一件不應該做的事，或是說了不恰當的話，且對方有意識到你的不高興時，就會跟你說對不起、不好意思等請你原諒的話，而如果你覺得那是無傷大雅的，或不想讓場面很尷尬(即使你心裡還是會生氣或在意)，那麼你就可以跟對方說這句話。

情境對話1：

Ⓐ I am sorry that I shouted at you.
對不起，我對你大叫.

Ⓑ Forget it. I don't remember it.
算了。我不記得了。

情境對話2：

Ⓐ I feel so sorry to interrupt your conversation with your boss.
對於打斷你跟你老闆之間的對話，我感到很抱歉。

Ⓑ Forget it. He won't mind.
算了。他不會介意的。

字　彙

interrupt 中斷；打擾	conversation 對話
boss 老闆	mind 介意

98. Get over yourself.

別自以為是。

說　明

　若某個人很自戀或容易自我感覺良好時，你就可以跟他說這句話。但對象通常會用在較熟的友人之間。

情境對話1：

Ⓐ I'm pretty charming, right?
我很有魅力，你說是不是？

Ⓑ Get over yourself.
別自以為是。

情境對話2：

Ⓐ I think I am the only one who is qualified enough to attend this contest.
我想我是唯一夠資格參加這項比賽的人。

Ⓑ Get over yourself. Betty is much better than you.
別自以為是。貝蒂比你還優。

字 彙

pretty 非常;漂亮	charming 有魅力的
qualify 有資格	attend 參加
better 比~還更好	

99. Get to the point.

說重點。

說 明

當別人所敘述的話語過於冗長或無重點時,就可以跟對方說這句話。

情境對話1:

Ⓐ ...So, in my opinion, we should make more efforts to protect the environment, then...

……所以,依我之見,我們應該更努力來設法保護環境,然後……

Ⓑ Gary, please get to the point.

蓋瑞,請說重點。

情境對話2:

Ⓐ We're now in a hurry, so get to the point.

我們現在很匆忙,你就說重點吧。

Ⓑ Ok, I get it.

好,了解。

字 彙

opinion 意見	effort 努力
protect 保護	environment 環境
hurry 趕緊;催促	

100. Go ahead.

(050)

你請便。/去做吧！

說　明

　　當你對於對方所提的建議沒有什麼意見時，就可以跟他說這句話。另外，若你的朋友到你家時，如果他想要借廁所或借用其他物品時，或是有其他要求時，倘若你也不介意，也可以用這句話表示。另外，若你支持某人所想做的決定時，也可以跟他說這句話。

情境對話1：

🅐 May I use the bathroom?
我可以借用廁所嗎？

🅑 Yes, go ahead. Turn right at the corner and you can see it.
可以啊，請便。在那個牆角右轉你就可以看到了。

情境對話2：

🅐 If you would like to do it, then just go ahead!
如果你想做的話，那就去做吧！

🅑 Thanks for your support.
謝謝你的支持。

字　彙

bathroom 廁所；浴室　　　　corner 角落
support 支持

101. Go straight.

直走。

說　明

　　一直往前走路，就叫做 Go straight.

情境對話1：

🅐 Excuse me. Do you know how to go to the history museum?
不好意思。你知道歷史博物館怎麼走嗎？

🅑 Yes. Go straight and turn right at the traffic light then you can see it.
知道。直走然後在那個紅綠燈右轉，你就可以看到了。

情境對話2：

🅐 How do I get there?
我該怎麼到那邊？

🅑 Go straight and you'll see the sign. Follow the sign and you'll get there.
直走然後你會看到一個標誌。跟著標誌走你就會到那裡了。

字　彙

history 歷史　　　　　　　museum 博物館
traffic light 紅綠燈

102. Good news.

好消息。

說　明

當你聽到一件好消息時，就可以用這句話告訴別人。

情境對話1：

🅐 Good news!
好消息！

🅑 What is it?
什麼好消息？

Ⓐ I got the scholarship!
我得到獎學金了！

情境對話2：

Ⓐ I feel so upset because my cat, Oliver, just died last night.
我覺得好難過，因為我的貓，奧利佛昨晚死掉了。

Ⓑ Don't be sad. At least, I have good news for you.
別難過。至少，我有一個好消息給你。

字　彙

scholarship 獎學金　　　　upset 難過的
sad 傷心的

103. Haste makes waste.

欲速則不達。

說　明

　當你看到或聽到你的友人很著急或焦慮的忙著處理事情，而你擔心他會因此搞砸事情時，就可以用這句話勸他。

情境對話1：

Ⓐ Hurry! I need to hand in the report to Dr. Smith before tomorrow.
快點！我必須在明天之前把報告交給史密斯教授。

Ⓑ Haste makes waste.
欲速則不達。

情境對話2：

Ⓐ Haste makes waste. So, finish your work with carefulness.
欲速則不達。所以請細心謹慎地完成你的工作。

Ⓑ Ok, I got it.
好，我知道了。

字　彙

hand in 繳交　　　　　　　　carefulness 細心；謹慎

104. **He always talks big.**

他總是吹牛。

說　明

　當你發覺你認識的朋友裡，有人講話愛誇大、吹牛時，而有人不知道他是這樣的人時，就可以用這句話告訴其他人。當然，主詞可以隨著說話的對象而改變。例如，你也可以直接跟愛吹牛的當事人說 You always talk big!

情境對話1：

Ⓐ Don't believe what he says.
不要相信他說的話。

Ⓑ Why?
為什麼？

Ⓐ Because he always talks big.
因為他總是吹牛。

情境對話2：

Ⓐ Terry is not trustworthy.
泰瑞不值得信賴。

Ⓑ Yes, I do think so. He always talks big.
沒錯，我也這麼認為。他總是吹牛。

字　彙

trustworthy 可信的

105. He came by bus.

他搭公車來。

說 明

此句的重點在於 by bus。by 加上交通工具，即代表搭乘該交通工具。例如，by car(搭車)、by train(搭火車)、by taxi(搭計程車)⋯⋯等等。也等於 take a/an/the ＋交通工具名稱。

情境對話1：

Ⓐ How did Henry come here?
亨利怎麼來這裡的？

Ⓑ He came by bus.
他搭公車來的。

情境對話2：

Ⓐ It took him two hours to arrive in our city.
他花了兩小時到我們這城市。

Ⓑ How come?
為什麼？

Ⓐ Because he came by bus.
因為他搭公車。

字 彙

arrive 抵達

106. He is just a child.

(053)

他只是個孩子。

說 明

當你看到或聽到某個大人在指責其小孩的不是時，就可以跟他說這句話，讓他知道對方只是個小孩，不是故意做錯事的，或是不要跟小孩過不去、計較等等之意。

情境對話1：

Ⓐ He is just a child. Don't be so harsh on him.
他只是個孩子。別對他太嚴苛。

Ⓑ No. I have to teach him what"honesty"means!
不。我必須教他什麼是"誠實"。

情境對話2：

Ⓐ He threw the toys everywhere. I am so angry!
他把玩具到處亂丟。我真的很生氣！

Ⓑ He is just a child. He didn't mean to do it.
他只是個孩子。他不是故意的。

字　彙

harsh 嚴苛的	honesty 誠實
threw (throw 的過去式) 丟	everywhere 到處

107. He is looking for a job.

他在找工作。

說　明

此句重點在 look for(表示尋找)，後面可加任何名詞，表示在尋找某物。例如，I am looking for my watch.(我正在尋找我的手錶。)

情境對話1：

Ⓐ Why does he keep staring at the computer screen?
為什麼他一直盯著電腦銀幕？

Ⓑ He is looking for a job.
他在找工作。

情境對話2：

🅐 He is looking for a job so he can't go out with us.
他在找工作所以無法跟我們出去。

🅑 That's a pity.
真是可惜。

字　彙

stare 盯著；凝視　　　　　　screen 銀幕

pity 可惜；憐憫

---

108. He is my age.　　　

他跟我同歲。

說　明

　當你知道某人跟你同歲數時，就可以用這句話表示。主詞和比較的對象也可以替換，例如，**Kelly is her age.**(凱莉跟她同歲。)

情境對話1：

🅐 How old is Ryan?
萊恩幾歲？

🅑 He is my age.
他跟我同歲。

情境對話2：

🅐 Sam looks younger than you.
山姆看起來比你年輕。

🅑 Really? But he is my age.
真的嗎？但他跟我同歲。

字　彙

age 年齡　　　　　　younger 較年輕的

than 比

109. Help yourself.

自行取用。

說　明

當你的親友到你家拜訪或作客時，就可以用這句話告知對方，表示一種客氣，讓對方感到比較自在、不受拘束。當然，地點不侷限在家中，也可以是你熟悉的處所，例如，公司辦公室。

情境對話1：

Ⓐ Can I have some water?
我可以喝點水嗎？

Ⓑ Of course. Help yourself.
當然。你就自行取用。

情境對話2：

Ⓐ Benny, help yourself if you'd like to have something to eat.
班尼，如果你想吃東西的話就自己拿吧。

Ⓑ Ok. Thanks a lot!
好。多謝了！

字　彙

water 水　　　　　　　　　yourself 你自己

would like 想要

110. Here comes the bus.

公車來了。

說　明

此句重點在於 Here comes 加上某個名詞，表示某個東西來了。例如，Here comes the train.(火車來了。)、Here comes your meal.(你點的餐來了。)

情境對話1：

Ⓐ Eric, here comes the bus.
艾瑞克，公車來了。

Ⓑ Ok. Bye, mom.
好。再見了，媽。

情境對話2：

Ⓐ Here comes the bus!
公車來了！

Ⓑ Let's get on the bus.
我們上車吧！

字　彙

get on 上車

---

111. **Here you are.**

給你。

說　明

　此句通常用在店員和顧客之間的對話，例如，你去速食餐廳點餐，店員將你的餐點送來時，他就會跟你說這句話。當然，這也可用在一般朋友之間的對話上，例如，你把某個東西給對方時，就可以說 Here you are. 或是 Here it is.

情境對話1：

Ⓐ I want a large ice Latte, but no ice.
我要一杯大杯的冰拿鐵，去冰。

Ⓑ Here you are, sir.
先生，你的冰拿鐵好了。

情境對話2：

Ⓐ Here you are. Three cheese burgers and two apple pies.
喏，你要的東西在這裡。三份起司漢堡和兩個蘋果派。

Ⓑ Thank you.
謝謝。

字　彙

large 大的	ice 冰
Latte 拿鐵	cheese 起司
burger 漢堡	pie 派

112. Hold on.　(056)

等一下！

說　明

　此句通常用在電話中。當某人打來時，但他所要找的人並未接此通電話，你就可以用這句話告訴對方，請他等一下。所以在電話中要請對方等一下時，就可以用這句話取代 wait。

情境對話1：

Ⓐ Hold on. I'll call Vincent now.
等一下。我現在去叫文森。

Ⓑ It's ok. I'll call him later.
沒關係。我待會再打給他。

情境對話2：

Ⓐ This is Watson speaking. Is Kate there?
我是華森。請問凱特在嗎？

Ⓑ Yes, she is. Hold on a second, please.
她在。請等一下。

字　彙

hold 保持；握住　　　　　　speak 講話
second 第二的；秒

113. Hurry up!

快一點！

說　明

　　當你發覺時間來不及，或情況緊急時，而對方還在拖拖拉拉時，就
可以用這句話催促他快一點。

情境對話1：

Ⓐ Hurry up! You are late for school!
　　快一點！你上學要遲到了！

Ⓑ Ok! I know.
　　好！我知道了。

情境對話2：

Ⓐ When does the movie begin?
　　這部電影幾點演？

Ⓑ 10:00 a.m.
　　早上十點。

Ⓐ We only have five minutes. Hurry up!
　　我們只剩五分鐘了。快一點！

字　彙

late 遲到　　　　　　　　　begin 開始
only 僅只；唯一

114. I'm fine.

> 我很好，沒事。

說 明

當你心情不好或身體有受傷、不適時，你的朋友就會關心慰問你的情況，這時你就可以説這句話，請對方不用擔心。

情境對話1：

Ⓐ Are you ok, Sandra?
妳還好嗎？珊卓？

Ⓑ Yes, I'm fine.
嗯，我很好。

情境對話2：

Ⓐ I'm fine. Don't worry.
我很好。不用擔心。

Ⓑ Are you sure?
你確定嗎？

字 彙

worry 擔心

115. I'm full.

> 我飽了。

說 明

當你吃的很飽，但仍有人想邀你繼續吃或喝東西時，你就可以用這句話告訴他，你已經吃不下了。有時候，當你吃到不喜歡的東西時，也可以用這句話來委婉的婉拒對方。

情境對話1：

Ⓐ I'm full. I can't eat anymore.
　我飽了。我再也吃不下任何東西了。

Ⓑ What did you eat?
　你到底吃了什麼？

情境對話2：

Ⓐ Do you want more rice?
　你想再多來點飯嗎？

Ⓑ No, thanks. I'm full.
　不了，謝謝。我飽了。

字　彙

full 充滿的；飽的　　　　　anymore 再也不
rice 飯

116. I'm home.

我到家了。

說　明

　如果你是跟家人或其他友人一起居住時，你回家時就可用這句話來
與家人或朋友打聲招呼。告知他你已經回來了。

情境對話1：

Ⓐ I'm home, mom.
　我到家了，媽。

Ⓑ Good. Come to have dinner!
　很好。來吃晚餐吧！

情境對話2：

Ⓐ Finally, I'm home.
我終於到家了。

Ⓑ You look so tired.
你看起來很累。

Ⓐ Because I worked overtime again today.
因為我今天又加班。

字 彙

finally 最後；終於

tired 疲累的

overtime 加班；超時

117. I'm in a hurry!

我在趕時間!

說 明

當你忙著處理某件緊急的事情時，或是趕車、趕寄信件之類的事情時，而對方還不知道你的狀況時，就可以用這句話跟對方表示你真的很忙或急著做某事。

情境對話1：

Ⓐ Why do you look so nervous?
為什麼你看起很緊張？

Ⓑ I'm in a hurry !
我在趕時間哪！

情境對話2：

Ⓐ I'm in a hurry. Could you please give me a ride to the train station?
我在趕時間。你可以載我到火車站嗎？

B Sure, come on.
當然，走吧。

字 彙

nervous 緊張的   ride 乘坐；搭乘

station 站

---

118. I'm lost.

我迷路了。

說 明

　　當你在人生地不熟的地方迷路時，就可以用這句話請當地人或警察幫忙你找到正確的路。此外，這句話另有其意，即"我迷失了。"用來表示自己對於目前的狀態或人生目標正處於一種茫然的情況。

情境對話1：

A Why are you crying, little girl?
小女孩，妳為什麼哭呢？

B I'm lost.
我迷路了。

情境對話2：

A Excuse me. Can you show me the way to this hotel? I'm lost.
請問一下。你可以告訴我怎麼到這家旅館嗎？我迷路了。

B Sorry, I'm not a local resident.
不好意思，我不是當地人。

字 彙

show 指示   hotel 旅館；飯店

local 本地的   resident 居民

119. I'm not sure.

我不確定。

說　明

當別人問你問題時，而你不確定該事的答案或該如何處理時，就可以用這句話告訴對方。

情境對話1：

Ⓐ I'm not sure if my answer is correct or not.
我不確定我的答案是不是對的。

Ⓑ Then, who should I turn to?
那我該找誰呢？

情境對話2：

Ⓐ Will Matt come here?
麥特會來嗎？

Ⓑ I'm not sure.
我不確定。

字　彙

if 如果　　　　　　　　　　correct 正確的；糾正

turn to 求助於

120. I'm on a diet.

我在節食。

說　明

當別人想邀你吃東西時，可是你正在控制飲食的時候，就可以用這句話。或者也可以說 I'm losing weight. (我正在減肥中。)

情境對話1：

Ⓐ Why are you eating less?
你怎麼吃這麼少？

Ⓑ I'm on a diet.
我在節食。

情境對話2：

Ⓐ I'm on a diet now so don't invite me to any restaurant.
我正在節食所以不要找我去餐廳吃飯。

Ⓑ But we have a reunion this Friday and the restaurant is really nice!
但這星期五我們有個聚會，而且那間餐廳真的很棒！

字　彙

less 較少(小)	diet 飲食
invite 邀請	reunion 重聚；聚會

121. I'm single.

我單身。

說　明

當別人問你婚姻狀況時，若是未婚者，就可以用這句話回答。

情境對話1：

Ⓐ Are you married?
你結婚了嗎？

Ⓑ No, I'm single.
不，我單身。

情境對話2：

Ⓐ I'm single so I can enjoy my free time more.
因為我單身所以有更多時間可以好好享受。

Ⓑ But, don't you want to have someone to accompany you?
但是，難道你不想找個人陪嗎？

字　彙

enjoy　享受

122. I could hardly speak.

我簡直說不出話來。

說　明

當你碰到某件讓你驚訝的事情時，不論是好或壞，只要讓你震驚到不知該用什麼措辭形容時，就可以用這句話表示你的訝異。

情境對話1：

Ⓐ Look at this picture. I could hardly speak.
你看這張照片。我簡直說不出話來。

Ⓑ Wow! Me, too.
哇！我也是！

情境對話2：

Ⓐ I could hardly speak when I saw the news. How could he do such a cruel thing?
我看到電視時簡直說不出話來。他怎麼可以做出令人髮指的事呢？

Ⓑ He should be sentenced to death!
應該要判他死刑！

字　彙

picture 圖片	hardly 幾乎不
cruel 殘忍的	sentence 判刑；句子
death 死亡	

123. I doubt it.

我懷疑。

說　明

當你對某件事情抱持懷疑的態度時，就可以用這句話。

情境對話1：

Ⓐ About this case, I doubt it.
關於這件案子，我非常懷疑。

Ⓑ Why do you say so?
怎麼說呢？

Ⓐ There were many suspicious parts unsolved.
因為有太多尚未釐清的疑點了。

情境對話2：

Ⓐ Jason said that he could complete Mr. William's designated assignment.
傑生說他能完成威廉先生指定的任務。

Ⓑ Well, I doubt it.
這我倒是很懷疑。

字　彙

suspicious 懷疑的	unsolved 未解決的
complete 完成	designated 指定的

124. I have the right to know. (061)

我有權知道。

說　明

當你想知道某件事情的來龍去脈時，可是對方卻不願告訴你時，你就可以用這句話告訴對方，但前提是要讓對方相信你真的有權利知道該事，否則對方不會輕易告訴你他所想隱瞞的事情。

情境對話1：

Ⓐ I'm the person involved in this event. Thus, I have the right to know.
我是這事件的當事人。所以，我有權知道。

Ⓑ Ok, if you insist.
好吧，如果你堅持的話。

情境對話2：

Ⓐ You don't have the slightest right to know what happened to my son!
你根本沒有權利知道我兒子所發生的事！

Ⓑ Of course I have the right to know! I'm his father!
我當然有權利知道！我是孩子的爸！

字　彙

person 人	involved 牽連(相關)的
event 事件	thus 因此
right 權利	insist 堅持
slightest 最微量；最輕微的	son 兒子

125. I get the picture.

我明白了。

說　明

　此句等同於 I understand. /I see. /I get it.等說法。通常用在對方跟你敘述某件事情時，而你了解他所指的意思後，就可以跟他說 I get the picture.表示你懂了。

情境對話1：

Ⓐ Now, do you understand it?
　現在，你瞭解了嗎？

Ⓑ Yes, I get the picture.
　是的，我明白了。

情境對話2：

Ⓐ I get the picture about what you explained. Then, what's the next step?
　我明白你所解釋的了。那麼，下一步呢？

Ⓑ I don't know. I need time to think about it well.
　我不知道。我需要時間好好思考。

字　彙

step 步驟

126. I have a runny nose. 062

我一直流鼻水。

說　明

　此句話也可以說 My nose is running.

情境對話1：

Ⓐ I have a runny nose.
我一直流鼻水。

Ⓑ Then you'll need tissues.
那麼你會需要很多衛生紙。

情境對話2：

Ⓐ I have had a runny nose all day long.
我一整天都在流鼻水。

Ⓑ Why don't you see a doctor?
你為什麼不去看醫生？

字　彙

tissue 衛生紙　　　　　　　　all day long 整天
doctor 醫生

127. I have a surprise for you.

我有一個驚喜要給你。

說　明

當你想給對方一個意想不到的驚喜時，就可以跟他說這句話。

情境對話1：

Ⓐ Carol, close your eyes.
凱若，把眼睛閉上。

Ⓑ Why?
為什麼？

Ⓐ Just do what I say. I have a surprise for you.
照我說的做就是了。我有一個驚喜要給你。

情境對話2：

Ⓐ I have a surprise for you, mom!
媽，我有一個驚喜要給你喔！

Ⓑ What did you do again?
你又做了什麼事？

Ⓐ Don't worry. It's great news!
別擔心。是個很棒的好消息啦！

字　彙

close 關閉　　　　　　　　　　eye(s)眼睛
surprise 驚喜

128. I have no choice.

我別無選擇。

說　明

　當你身處進退兩難或很危急的情況下，而必須做出不得已的決定時，就可以用這句話告訴對方，以示你真的無計可施，只好做出一個勉為其難的決定，而此決定不一定會被眾人認同或接受，但卻是自己當下所能做的最好的決定。

情境對話1：

Ⓐ Sorry, but I have no choice. I have to end this relationship.
對不起，但我別無選擇。我必須結束這段關係。

Ⓑ No, we can start over again.
不，我們可以重新再來啊！

情境對話2：

Ⓐ I have no choice. I can't help you. Please forgive me.
我別無選擇。我無法幫你。請你原諒我。

B It's ok. I understand your dilemma.
沒關係。我知道你很為難。

字　彙

choice 選擇	end 結束
relationship 關係	start 開始
forgive 原諒	dilemma 兩難；困境

129. I love this game.

我愛這遊戲。

說　明

當你很愛某個你在玩或玩過的遊戲時，就可以用這句話告訴別人，或者也能讓別人對你所說的遊戲感到興趣。

情境對話1：

A I love this game so much! It's so interesting!
我很愛這遊戲！它真是太有趣了！

B Is it?
真的嗎？

情境對話2：

A Do you like this game?
你喜歡這遊戲嗎？

B Yes. I love this game. I play it almost every moment.
喜歡。我愛這遊戲。我幾乎無時無刻都在玩。

字　彙

interesting 有趣的	almost 幾乎
moment 時刻	

130. **I made it!**

(064)

我做到了！

說　明

　　當你費盡千辛萬苦，或經過嘔心瀝血的努力，終於達成目標或任務時，就可以用上這句話。

情境對話1：

Ⓐ I made it! I passed the application of the university.
我做到了！我通過這間大學的申請了！

Ⓑ Cool! I feel so happy for you!
太帥了！我真為你感到高興！

情境對話2：

Ⓐ It's unbelievable! I made it on my own!
真是難以相信！我居然自己可以做到！

Ⓑ I've told you already that I knew you could do it!
我早就告訴你我知道你可以的！

字　彙

application 申請	university 大學
unbelievable 難以置信的	already 已經

131. **I promise.**

我保證。

說　明

　　當你跟對方承諾或約定某件事情時，就可以用這句話跟對方擔保自己能實踐所約定或承諾的事情。

情境對話1：

Ⓐ I promise I will cope with this business smoothly.
我保證我會順利地處理好這樁生意。

Ⓑ I hope you will, too.
我也希望你可以處理好。

情境對話2：

Ⓐ Can you promise you will treat her well?
你可以保證你會好好對待她嗎？

Ⓑ Yes, I can. I promise I will treat her well till the end of the world.
是的，我可以。我保證我會好好對待她直到世界末日。

字　彙

cope 處理	business 生意
treat 對待	till 直到

132. **I quit.** 065

我不幹了。

說　明

　當你受夠目前的工作而意欲辭職時，就可以跟老闆這麼說。所以quit是自己要辭職，而不是fired被開除。另外，針對自己目前所進行的事情或任務，覺得太難無法勝任或達成目標時，也可以用這句話代表放棄、不做的意思。

情境對話1：

Ⓐ I'm going to tell my boss that I quit tomorrow.
我明天要告訴我的老闆我不幹了。

Ⓑ Are you serious?
你是認真的嗎？

情境對話2：

Ⓐ I quit! I can't do it by myself.
我放棄！我無法獨自完成這事。

Ⓑ Maybe you just need to take a rest.
也許你只是需要休息一下而已

字　彙

quit 辭職；放棄　　　　　maybe 也許

133. I think so.

我也這麼想。

說　明

當你對他人的看法感到贊同時，就可以用這句話表示。

情境對話1：

Ⓐ I think we should cooperate to get the work done quickly.
我認為我們應該一起同心協力把這工作快點做完。

Ⓑ I think so.
我也這麼想。

情境對話2：

Ⓐ About the resolution to this project, I think so.
關於這計畫的解決方案，我也是這麼想。

Ⓑ Then, shall we act now?
那麼，我們現在可以開始行動嗎？

字　彙

cooperate 合作　　　　　done 完成的

quickly 快點　　　　　act 行動

134. I've got to go.

我該走了。

說　明

　當時間來不及，或是因應當時情況之故，而必須離開當時的現場時，就可以跟對方説這句話。

情境對話 1：

Ⓐ What time is it?
現在幾點了？

Ⓑ It's eight o'clock.
現在八點了。

Ⓐ Oops! I've got to go. I have a date.
噢！我該走了。我還有約。

情境對話 2：

Ⓐ I've got to go or I will be late for the conference.
我該走了否則會議會遲到。

Ⓑ Ok, see you next time.
好，那下次見。

字　彙

conference 會議

135. It depends.

那要看情況。

說　明

　當你不確定某活動或行程、事情能否如期完成時，就可以用這句話。又或者是，對於某些較難回答的問題，無法給予肯定的答案時，也可以用這句話來表示事情可能會有所變數或迂迴。完整句子為 It depends on the situation.

情境對話1：
Ⓐ Can we go on a picnic this Saturday?
這週六我們可以去野餐嗎？

Ⓑ It depends on the weather.
這取決於天氣。

情境對話2：
Ⓐ What will you do next？
你下一步要怎麼做？

Ⓑ I don't know. It depends.
我不知道。那要看情況。

字　彙

picnic 野餐　　　　　　　　　　weather 天氣

---

136. It hurts.

067

(傷口)疼。

說　明

當你受傷時，無論是身體或心理上的，都可以用這句話表示。主詞 it 可以改成任何身體部位名稱，或是代表心，例如，心痛。

情境對話1：
Ⓐ Are you ok? How about your leg?
你還好嗎？你的腿怎麼了？

Ⓑ It hurts.
很痛。

情境對話2：
Ⓐ My heart hurts every time when I think of him.
每當想到他時我的心就會痛。

B Time will heal.
時間會療傷的。

字　彙

leg 腿　　　　　　　　　heart 心
heal 治癒

137. It matters a lot to me.

那對我很重要。

說　明

　某件事情對你而言很重要時，儘管旁人不這麼認為，就可以用這句話告訴對方你對該事的重視程度。

情境對話1：

A I have to attend that contest. It matters a lot to me.
我必須參加那場比賽。那對我很重要。

B I'll back you up if you have to.
我會支持你的，如果你一定要參加的話。

情境對話2：

A Why do you always bring this ring with you?
為什麼你總是隨身帶著這只戒指？

B It matters a lot to me. My mom gave it to me before she left.
它對我很重要。我媽在離開之前把這只戒指給了我。

字　彙

back up 支持　　　　　　ring 戒指

138. It really takes time.

這樣太耽誤時間了。

說 明

　若某人提出的意見會導致一場約會或行程延誤時，就可以跟他說這句話，然後再解釋原因給他聽。

情境對話1：

Ⓐ It really takes time if we do so.
如果我們這麼做的話就太耽誤時間了。

Ⓑ But that's the only way we can do it.
但那是我們唯一能做的了。

情境對話2：

Ⓐ Why don't we pick up Sandy first then go to see a movie later?
為什麼我們不先接珊迪然後再去看電影呢？

Ⓑ It really takes time.
這樣太耽誤時間了。

字 彙

pick up 接　　　　　　　　theater 戲院

139. It's a deal!

一言為定！

說 明

　當你與對方約好或承諾某件事情時，為了表示真能做到所約定的事情，就可以說這句話。所以當你跟別人說這句話時，就一定要做到，否則別人不會再輕易相信。

情境對話1：

Ⓐ Let's meet at the department store at noon tomorrow.
我們明天中午就約在這家百貨公司碰面。

Ⓑ Ok, it's a deal!
好，一言為定！

情境對話2：

Ⓐ Do you like badminton?
你喜歡羽毛球嗎？

Ⓑ Yes, I do.
喜歡呀！

Ⓐ Then, how about playing badminton together at the gym this Sunday noon?
那這星期日中午在體育館一起打羽毛球如何？

Ⓑ Sure. It's a deal!
好啊。一言為定！

字　彙

department store　百貨公司	noon　正午
badminton　羽毛球	gym　體育館

140. It's a long story.

 069

說來話長。

說　明

　　當你應某人要求敘述一件事情的起因時，而你覺得這解釋會花不少時間時，就可以告訴對方說 It's a long story 說來話長，此時就可以視對方反應(想聽或不想聽)，以決定要解釋與否。

情境對話1：

Ⓐ Why does Kelly look so sad?
為什麼凱莉看起來這麼難過？

Ⓑ Well, it's a long story.
這說來話長。

情境對話2：

Ⓐ How did this car accident happen?
這場車禍是怎麼發生的？

Ⓑ Are you sure you want to know? It's a long story after all.
你確定你想知道嗎？畢竟這說來話長喔！

字　彙

story 故事　　　　　　　　happen 發生

---

141. It's a piece of cake.

那真是輕而易舉。

說　明

　　當別人有問題請教你或想麻煩你幫忙時，若你覺得該事很簡單或不會對你造成任何困擾時，就可以告訴對方這句話，表示你會幫他這個忙。

情境對話1：

Ⓐ I don't understand this question.
我不懂這個題目。

Ⓑ It's a piece of cake. Let me explain it.
這很簡單。讓我解釋給你聽吧。

情境對話2：

A David, could you please give me a ride to my home? Will that bother you?

大衛，可以請你載我回家嗎？這樣會不會打擾到你呀？

B Not at all. It's a piece of cake.

一點也不。這事很輕而易舉。

字　彙

bother 打擾

142. It's getting cold.

變冷了。

說　明

當天氣變冷時，就可以用到這句話。有時也可以用來當作一開始對話時的開頭。而這裡的 it 則是指天氣。

情境對話1：

A It's getting cold.

天氣變冷了。

B Yeah. Winter seems to be approaching.

是啊。冬天似乎到了。

情境對話2：

A You'd better put on a coat. It's getting cold.

你最好多穿一件外套。天氣變冷了。

B But I don't feel cold.

但我不覺得冷。

字　彙

| winter 冬天 | approaching 接近；來臨 |
| put on 穿上 | coat 外套 |

143. It's raining cats and dogs.

下大雨。

說　明

此句也可以說成 It rains a lot./ It rains heavily./ It's raining heavily./ The rain is heavy. 皆表示雨下得非常大。

情境對話1：

Ⓐ Wow, it's raining cats and dogs!
哇，雨下得可真大！

Ⓑ Oh, no! I didn't bring the umbrella.
喔，不！我沒有帶傘。

情境對話2：

Ⓐ Ted, how's the weather outside?
泰德，外面天氣如何？

Ⓑ It's raining cats and dogs outside.
外面正在下大雨。

字　彙

| umbrella 雨傘 |
| outside 外面 |

144. It's too good to be true!

好得難以置信。

說　明

　當你得知某件事情或是消息好的難以相信時，好比從天而降的好運或禮物時，就可以用上這句話。

情境對話1：

Ⓐ Do you believe, Peter? You just won the election!
　你相信嗎，彼得？你剛贏得這次的選舉！

Ⓑ Really? It's too good to be true!
　真的嗎？這真是好到令人難以置信！

情境對話2：

Ⓐ It's too good to be true that I won the lottery!
　這真是好到令人難以置信，我竟然中了樂透！

Ⓑ Oh my god! You are so lucky!
　我的天呀！你真是太幸運了！

字　彙

election 選舉　　　　　　　lottery 樂透
lucky 幸運的

145. It's up to you.

看你的決定囉！

說　明

　當別人問你的看法時，你也提供自己的意見供對方參考，但沒有一定要對方採取你的意見時，就可以跟對方說 It's up to you. 以示決定權還是在對方身上。若到時對方對於結果不滿意時，也不會把責任歸咎到你身上。

情境對話1：

Ⓐ Do I have to attend the feast?
我一定得參加那場宴會嗎？

Ⓑ It's up to you!
看你的決定囉！

情境對話2：

Ⓐ Which sweater suits me?
哪件毛衣適合我？

Ⓑ It's up to you. You can try them on first.
這取決於你。你可以先試穿他們。

字　彙

feast 盛宴　　　　　　　　　　sweater 毛衣
try on 試穿

---

146. It's your turn.　　🎧072

輪到你。

說　明

　當對方不知道某事情或活動輪到他時，就可以跟他說這句話。但有時對方知道輪到自己，你也可以這麼說，讓他知道真的輪到他自己。

情境對話1：

Ⓐ Tina, it's your turn.
蒂娜，輪到你了。

Ⓑ Ok, thanks.
好，謝謝。

情境對話2：

Ⓐ It's your turn to enter the classroom for the oral test.
輪到你進教室口試了。

Ⓑ I know. I'm so nervous.
我知道。我好緊張。

字　彙

oral　口說的

---

147. I'll be along later.

我隨後就到。

說　明

當對方呼叫你時，但你因有事耽擱或要先處理事情，就可以跟他說這句話，請他先走，例如去參加聚會或開會之類等。

情境對話1：

Ⓐ Wells, I have something to deal with. I'll be along later.
威爾斯，我還有事要處理。我隨後就到。

Ⓑ Ok, see you later.
好，那待會見。

情境對話2：

Ⓐ Taylor, let's go!
泰勒，我們走吧！

Ⓑ Wait! I'll be along later.
等一下！我隨後就來。

字　彙

deal with　處理

148. I'll be right there.

(073)

我馬上就到。

說 明

此句之意類似 I'll be along later.(我隨後到)。後面可以加時間，例如，in five minutes(五分鐘內)。

情境對話1：

Ⓐ I'll be right there, Ben. I need to make a call to Amy.
班，我馬上就到。我得打通電話給艾咪。

Ⓑ Alright. Don't talk too long.
好吧。別講太久。

情境對話2：

Ⓐ Sam, your wife was sent to the hospital to deliver the baby.
山姆，你太太被送到醫院要待產了。

Ⓑ Ok! I'll be right there in ten minutes!
好！我十分鐘內就會到！

字 彙

make a call 打電話	hospital 醫院
alright 好吧	deliver 遞送；生(孩子)

149. I'll be back soon.

我馬上回來。

說 明

原本你在現場可能和朋友、家人或同事一起，但臨時有事要處理，而需要離開現場，就可以跟對方說這句話。

情境對話1：

Ⓐ I'll be back soon. Don't go away!
我馬上回來。別走開！

Ⓑ Ok, I'll stay here.
好，我會待在這裡。

情境對話2：

Ⓐ Where are you going? The test will begin later.
你要去哪裡？考試等下就開始了。

Ⓑ OK, I'll be back soon.
好，我馬上回來。

字　彙

stay 停留；待

---

150. I'll do my best.

(074)

我會盡力而為。

說　明

當你不知道自己能否完成或克服一件任務或挑戰時，但至少會盡自己最大力量去做時，就可以用上這句話。

情境對話1：

Ⓐ Do you think you can conquer this challenge?
你覺得你可以征服這項挑戰嗎？

Ⓑ I'm not sure but I'll do my best.
我不確定但我會盡力而為。

情境對話2：

Ⓐ Don't worry. I'll do my best to rescue the people trapped in the mountains.
別擔心。我會盡力把困在山裡的人給救出來。

B Thank you very much.
非常感謝你。

字　彙

conquer 征服；克服	challenge 挑戰
rescue 拯救	mountain 山

151. I'll fix you up.

我會幫你打點的。

說　明

　這裡所說的打點是指幫認識的熟人，通常指家人及好朋友或是同事，處理好一些瑣事。因此這裡的 fix 不是指修理或維修的意思。

情境對話1：

A Fine. I'll fix you up well.
好。我會幫你打點好的。

B Thanks! You did me a great favor!
謝啦！你幫我一個大忙！

情境對話2：

A What can I do in this case?
這件案子我能做些什麼？

B I'll fix you up the rest of the files, so what you need to do is to track him.
我會整理好剩下的檔案，所以你所要做的就是跟蹤他。

字　彙

favor 恩惠	rest 剩下的
file 檔案	track 追蹤；跟蹤

152. I'll take this please.

(075)

我要這個。

說　明

當你在買東西時，看見所要選的物品時，就可以跟店員説這句話。

情境對話1：

Ⓐ I'll take this please.
我要這個。

Ⓑ Ok.
沒問題。

情境對話2：

Ⓐ How much does the earphone cost?
這耳機要多少錢？

Ⓑ Three hundred dollars.
三百元。

Ⓐ Then I'll take this please.
那我要這個。

字　彙

earphone 耳機

153. I'll think about it.

我會想一想。

說　明

對於某事的處理或解決方式，無法立即給予明確的答案時，就可以告訴對方這句話，表示你需要時間思考一下。另外，對方提供你不錯的條件時，但你需要時間思考其條件的利弊時，也可用這句話表示。

情境對話 1：

Ⓐ If I give you a raise in salary, would you consider staying?
如果我給你加薪，你會考慮留下來嗎？

Ⓑ I'll think about it. I'll reply to you tomorrow.
我會想一想。我明天會回覆你。

情境對話 2：

Ⓐ I'll think about it. After all, it's not easy to make a decision on this matter.
我會想一想。畢竟，這件事不是那麼容易就可以下決定的。

Ⓑ Right. I'll wait for your answer.
沒錯。我會等你的答案。

字　彙

raise 增加；提升	salary 薪水
consider 考慮	reply 回覆
decision 決定	

---

154. I'll think it over.

我會好好考慮的。

說　明

此句等於 I'll consider it./ I'll take it into account. 皆指我會好好考慮的。

情境對話 1：

Ⓐ I'll think it over about what to do next.
我會好好考慮下一步該怎麼做。

Ⓑ Good. You should have thought about it well.
很好。你早就該好好想一想了。

情境對話2：

Ⓐ It's not urgent now. You've got lots of time to think about it.
現在還沒有很急。你有很多時間好好想一想。

Ⓑ You're right. I'll think it over.
沒錯。我會好好考慮的。

字　彙

urgent 緊急的

155. Just between you and me.

這是我們之間的秘密。

說　明

　　如果某件事情你不想讓其他人知道，但還是得找一個你值得相信的人說時，就可以跟他說這句話，讓他知道要守密。

情境對話1：

Ⓐ Molly, I have something to tell you, but just between you and me.
茉莉，我有事跟你說，但只有我們知道而已。

Ⓑ Ok, I'll keep it secret.
好，我會保密的。

情境對話2：

Ⓐ About this matter, just between you and me. Don't tell anyone.
關於這件事，這是我們之間的秘密。別告訴任何人。

Ⓑ I know. I won't tell anyone.
我知道。我不會告訴其他人的。

字　彙

between 在~之間　　　　　　　secret 機密的；秘密

---

156. Keep in touch! 〔077〕

常保連絡。

說　明

　當你跟一位剛結交的朋友或是認識很久的朋友或同事要分離時，就可以跟他說這句話，以示之後可以再連絡。

情境對話1：

Ⓐ Hey, Jamie. Keep in touch.
嘿，傑米。要常保聯絡。

Ⓑ No problem. I'll write you letters.
沒問題。我會寫信給你。

情境對話2：

Ⓐ I'll leave for Australia next Monday.
我下週一要去澳洲。

Ⓑ Remember to keep in touch, my friend.
我的朋友，記得保持聯絡。

字　彙

write 寫
letter 信
Australia 澳洲

157. Let's call it a day.

今天到此為止吧。

說 明

當工作很累或想要把一件事情到此告一段落時，就可以用上這句話。

情境對話1：

Ⓐ Let's call it a day, everyone!
各位，今天到此為止吧！

Ⓑ Eventually, we can go home now.
我們現在終於可以回家了。

情境對話2：

Ⓐ I'm so exhausted, Kayson. Can we continue tomorrow?
凱森，我好累喔。我們明天再繼續好嗎？

Ⓑ Ok. Let's call it a day.
好吧。那今天就到此為止吧。

字 彙

eventually 最後；終於   exhausted 筋疲力竭的
continue 繼續

158. Let's get started.

開始幹活吧！

說 明

當要開始從事某件事情、任務或活動時，就可以用這句話以示開工。

情境對話1：

Ⓐ It's useless to discuss without action. Let's get started.
光討論不行動是沒用的。開始幹活吧。

Ⓑ That makes sense! Let's do it now!
説的有道理。那現在就開始吧！

情境對話2：

Ⓐ Let's get started before it gets dark!
天黑前趕緊幹活吧！

Ⓑ Right. It's more risky at night.
沒錯。晚上會更危險。

字 彙

useless 無用的	action 行動
dark 暗的	risky 危險的；冒險的

159. Let's see.

讓我們看看。

說 明

　　當你和友人一起時，發現有些狀況時，就可以跟同行者説這句話。或者，你為某件事物想辦法解決時，而欲知此方式是否有效時，也可以用上這句話。

情境對話1：

Ⓐ It seems that there's something in front of us.
我們前面好像有什麼東西似的。

Ⓑ Let's see. Sherry, give me a flashlight and the bat.
我們來看看吧。雪莉，給我一個手電筒和棍棒。

情境對話2：

Ⓐ Let's see if the machine works or not.
我們來看看這台機器會不會動。

Ⓑ Great! It works!
太棒了！它動了！

字　彙

flashlight 手電筒　　　　　　　　bat 棍棒

---

160. Let's take a break.

我們休息一下。

說　明

　當因為工作或上課到一個程度時，而覺得需要休息時，就可以用這句跟上司或老師反應。反之，若你是上司或老師，當你發現下屬或學生已經無法繼續工作或是聽課時，就可以跟他們說這句話，讓他們休息一下。

情境對話1：

Ⓐ Miss Sarah, let's take a break, shall we? We are so tired.
莎拉小姐，可以讓我們休息一下嗎？我們好累喔。

Ⓑ Ok. But only ten minutes.
好。但只有十分鐘。

情境對話2：

Ⓐ Let's take a break, everyone.
各位，我們休息一下吧。

Ⓑ Good. Finally I can finish my breakfast, now.
很好。我現在終於可以吃完我的早餐了。

字　彙

break 休息　　　　　　　　breakfast 早餐

161. Life is short.

人生苦短。

說　明

　此句也是另一種告訴人要把握時間的諺語，因此當你的友人不論是杞人憂天，或是無所事事的時候，就可用此句告訴他人生苦短，所以要把握當下。

情境對話1：

Ⓐ Life is short.
人生苦短。

Ⓑ That's right. So, let's have some fun now!
沒錯。所以我們現在來找樂子吧！

情境對話2：

Ⓐ Don't waste time on stupid and meaningless stuff. Life is short.
不要把時間浪費在愚蠢和沒意義的東西上。人生苦短。

Ⓑ Yeah, so what should we do now?
對，所以我們現在應該做什麼呢？

字　彙

fun 樂趣	waste 浪費
meaningless 無意義的	stuff 東西；事情

162. Like father like son.

有其父必有其子。

說　明

　這是一句常用的英文諺語，當你看見某男生所做的事就如同他父親的翻版時，不論是正面或負面的評論，都可以用這句話。

情境對話 1：

Ⓐ He always gets drunk and beats up his wife.
他總是喝醉酒還毆打老婆。

Ⓑ Like father like son.
有其父必有其子。

情境對話 2：

Ⓐ Well so goes the proverb, "Like father, like son."
俗話說的好：有其父必有其子

Ⓑ No wonder he loves his family so much.
難怪他這麼愛他的家人。

字　彙

beat up 痛打　　　　　　　　　proverb 俗諺

---

163. Make yourself at home.

甭客氣。

說　明

當有客人到家裡作客時，就可以用上這句話。

情境對話 1：

Ⓐ Jessie, just make yourself at home.
潔絲，你就甭客氣了。

Ⓑ I know. Thank you,
我知道了。謝謝你。

情境對話 2：

Ⓐ Relax. Make yourself at home.
放輕鬆，把這當作自己家一樣。

B Ok, but I still don't get used to it.
好，但我還是不太習慣。

字　彙
get used to 習慣

---

164. Me, too.

我也是。

說　明
　當對方說出其對某件事的看法時，或做出某些事情時，而你也有相同的看法或經驗時，就可以用這句話回應

情境對話 1：

A I strongly recommend David to be the candidate for next manager.
我強力推薦大衛為下一任經理候選人。

B Me, too. He is talented and responsible.
我也是。他聰敏又負責任。

情境對話 2：

A She said the service of the restaurant is nice. Is that true?
她說那家餐廳的服務很好。是真的嗎？

B That's right. Me, too. I've been there before.
沒錯。我也這麼認為。我曾經去過那家餐廳。

字　彙
strongly 強烈地　　　　　recommend 推薦
candidate 候選人　　　　talented 有天分的
responsible 負責的

165. Money talks.

有錢能使鬼推磨。

說　明

　這是一句英文諺語，可用來形容某些人的觀念就是認為只要能用錢解決的事，就會用這種方式去處理。

情境對話1：

Ⓐ I believe the saying" Money talks."
我相信"有錢能使鬼推磨"這句諺語。

Ⓑ But money isn't everything.
但錢不是萬能的。

情境對話2：

Ⓐ Since money talks, why don't you give him more pay?
既然有錢能使鬼推磨，為什麼你不多給他薪水？

Ⓑ He is not that kind of man you think.
他不是你想的那種人。

字　彙

pay 支付；報酬(薪資)　　　　kind 仁慈的

166. Move forward!

往前進。

說　明

　此句話通常用在一群人外出時，例如：帶學生郊遊，或導遊領隊時，若希望他們往前進到下一處時，就可以說這句話。

情境對話 1：

Ⓐ Please move forward, everyone. We are going to visit the National Palace Museum.
各位請往前進。我們將參觀國立故宮博物院。

Ⓑ Great! I've looked forward to it for so long.
太棒了！我已經期待好久了。

情境對話 2：

Ⓐ How far is the botanical garden from here?
植物園離這裡有多遠？

Ⓑ I think if we move forward quickly, it will appear in front of us soon.
我想如果我們快點前進的話，它不久就會出現在我們眼前。

字　彙

national 國立的	palace 宮殿
look forward to 期待	botanical 植物的
garden 花園	appear 出現

167. My mouth is watering.

我要流口水了。

說　明

當你看到某個讓你垂涎的食物時，就可以用上這句話。

情境對話 1：

Ⓐ My mouth is watering when I see something delicious.
每當我看見好吃的東西時我就會流口水。

Ⓑ Me, too.
我也是。

情境對話2：

Ⓐ What's wrong with you?
你怎麼了？

Ⓑ I smell the food and my mouth is watering now. I'm so hungry!
我聞到食物的味道而且要流口水了。我好餓！

字　彙

mouth-watering 流口水的　　delicious 美味的
smell 聞

---

168. My treat.
我請客。

說　明

當你心血來潮或忽然有錢進帳時，就可以跟你的朋友、家人或同事說這句話。

情境對話1：

Ⓐ I just got promoted today so it's my treat!
今天我剛升職所以我請客！

Ⓑ Hurray!
萬歲！

情境對話2：

Ⓐ The dish on the menu looks so great, but I think it also costs a lot.
菜單上的菜餚看起來好棒，但我想價格應該不斐。

🅑 Don't worry about the prices. My treat!
別擔心價錢。我請客！

字　彙

dish 菜餚；盤子　　　　　　　menu 菜單
price 價格

169. Never mind.

沒關係。

說　明

此句等同於 It's ok./Not at all.表示對於對方所做之事或行為，採取原諒或無所謂，沒關係的態度。

情境對話1：

🅐 Never mind. I'll clean the doghouse myself.
沒關係。我會自己清理狗屋。

🅑 Are you sure that you don't need any help?
你確定你不需要任何幫忙嗎？

情境對話2：

🅐 I'm so sorry I messed up your room.
我很抱歉弄亂你的房間。

🅑 Never mind.
沒關係。

字　彙

clean 清理　　　　　　　doghouse 狗屋
mess up 弄亂

170. No kidding.

我是說真的。

說　明

　　當別人對你所說的事情或看法持懷疑的態度時，就可以用這句話告訴他，表示你是認真的，不是在開玩笑的。此句最好用在熟人之間，而少用於較正式的場合上。

情境對話1：

Ⓐ No kidding, Hank. You really look handsome in a black suit.
漢克，我是說真的。你穿黑色西裝真的看起來很帥。

Ⓑ Thank you. You're so sweet.
謝謝你。你嘴真甜。

情境對話2：

Ⓐ Are you serious?
你是認真的嗎？

Ⓑ No kidding. I'll teach Jim a lesson.
我是說真的。我會給吉姆一個教訓。

字　彙

handsome 帥的	suit 套裝
sweet 甜的	lesson 教訓；課程

171. No pain no gain.

不勞而無獲。

說　明

　　此句為常用諺語之一。當你看到你的朋友、同事或家人為了某件事情煩惱，是因為不夠努力而導致無法達成其所要的目標時，就可以用這句話鼓勵或安慰他。

情境對話1：

Ⓐ Keep this saying"No pain no gain"in your mind and one day you'll succeed.

把"不勞而無獲"這句諺語牢記心中，總有一天你就會成功。

Ⓑ Ok, I'll keep it in mind.

好的，我會記在心中的。

情境對話2：

Ⓐ If I could make a fortune in a night, I wouldn't have to work hard anymore.

如果我可以一夜致富，我就再也不用辛苦工作了。

Ⓑ Stop daydreaming. Don't you know that "No pain no gain."?

別做白日夢了。難道你不知道"不勞而無獲"嗎？

字　彙

succeed 成功　　　　　　make a fortune 賺大錢

172. No problem!

沒問題！

說　明

當別人交付你完成一件任務或請你幫忙時，若你有信心能完成，就可以說這句話。但要說這句話前，最好先衡量自己的能力，若無法達成，則很容易失信於他人。

情境對話1：

Ⓐ Can you pay the loan you owed back to the bank?

你可以還清你欠銀行的貸款嗎？

Ⓑ No problem!

沒問題！

情境對話2：

Ⓐ No problem! You have my word.
沒問題！我保證！

Ⓑ I feel relieved to hear that.
聽到你這麼說我就感到放心了。

字　彙

loan　貸款　　　　　　　　relieved　放心的；寬慰的

---

173. Not yet.

還沒。

說　明

當別人問你完成或去處理完某件事了沒，若尚未完成時，就可以回對方這句話。

情境對話1：

Ⓐ Rika, have you finished your homework?
瑞卡，你寫完功課了嗎？

Ⓑ Not yet.
還沒。

情境對話2：

Ⓐ Not yet. My mom hasn't been to Hong Kong.
還沒。我媽媽還沒去過香港。

Ⓑ Well, you should take her there. It's a shopper's paradise.
那麼你應該帶她去那裡。它是個購物者的天堂。

字　彙

Hong Kong　香港　　　　　shopper　購物者
paradise　天堂

174. Of course.

當然。

說　明

　　當別人問你對於某事的看法，或是請你幫忙時，若你的想法與之相同，或是可以幫對方的忙時，就可以用上此句。

情境對話1：

🅐 Jack, can your dad fly an airplane?
傑克，你爸爸會開飛機嗎？

🅑 Of course.
當然。

情境對話2：

🅐 Do you remember him?
你記得他嗎？

🅑 Of course I do. He is the man who kidnapped my younger brother.
我當然記得。他就是綁架我弟弟的人。

字　彙

kidnap 綁架

175. One more chance, please.

請再給我一次機會。

說　明

　　當你因為做錯事情或某件任務失敗時，希望對方或上司再給你機會彌補時，就可以說這句話。

情境對話 1：

Ⓐ One more chance, please. I promise I'll compensate all the mistakes I made.

請再給我一次機會。我保證我會補償所有犯下的錯。

Ⓑ No, it's too late.

不，太遲了。

情境對話 2：

Ⓐ You ruined everything, including our friendship.

你毀了一切，還包含我們的友情。

Ⓑ One more chance, please. I didn't mean it.

請再給我一次機會。我不是有意的。

字　彙

compensate 補償　　　　　include 包含

friendship 友誼

176. One more time.

再一次。

說　明

　　當你的友人或同事、學生所做之事沒有達成該有的標準或目標時，就可以跟他說這句話，以示給他機會或鼓勵他再接再厲。另外，我們有時也會說，"如果你再一次這麼做的話，我就不要再……或是我就會……。" 此時的 **one more time** 也可用在其中。

情境對話 1：

Ⓐ I lost the opportunity of applying for the teaching position in that university.

我失去了申請在該所大學擔任教職的機會。

Ⓑ It's ok. You can still apply for it one more time.
沒關係。你還是可以再一次申請。

情境對話2：

Ⓐ Sean, if you do it one more time, I will definitely tell your parents!
尚恩，如果你再做一次的話，我絕對會告訴你的爸媽！

Ⓑ Ok, I'm sorry, Mr. Dennis.
是的，對不起，丹尼斯先生。

字　彙

opportunity 機會　　　　　position 職位；位置
parents 父母

177. Practice makes perfect.

熟能生巧。

說　明

當你的友人、同事或學生對於你的表現或某專業技能感到欽佩時，就可以用這句話回應，也是一種謙虛的態度。反之，你想要鼓勵對方達成他所想的標準或目標時，也可用上此句話。

情境對話1：

Ⓐ Gary, how did you make it? The painting looks so beautiful!
蓋瑞，你怎麼做到的？這幅畫看起來好美喔！

Ⓑ Practice makes perfect. I paint 8 hours a day every day.
熟能生巧。我每天畫八小時。

情境對話2：

A Practice makes perfect. Try hard and practice every day, then you can also make it

熟能生巧。努力嘗試且每天練習，你也可以做到的。.

B Well, I do hope so.

唉，我也希望如此。

字 彙

painting 繪畫作品　　　　　　practice 練習

---

178. **Raise your hand, please.**

請舉手。

說 明

通常此句用在學校或開會的場合，因為人數眾多，發言有限，所以需要舉手。或是你希望對方或群眾跟著你做動作時，也可以用上這句話。

情境對話1：

A Everyone, raise your hand, please. Follow my movement.

各位請舉手。跟著我的動作。

情境對話2：

A If you have any questions, raise your hand, please. Ok, Jenny, what's your question?

如果你有任何問題，請舉手。好的，珍妮，你有什麼問題？

B May I go to the bathroom?

我可以上廁所嗎？

字　彙

raise 舉起　　　　　　　　hand 手

movement 運動；動作

---

179. Read my lips.

你給我仔細聽好了。

說　明

　若有人對你的態度很不禮貌，或讓你有侵犯或不舒服的感覺時，就可以用這句話強烈回應，以表明你堅決的態度。另外，若對方真的聽不到或不懂你所說的話，也可以用這句話告訴他，請對方讀你的唇。

情境對話1：

🅐 Hey, you! Read my lips. Never step in my house again! Do you get it?

嘿，你！你給我仔細聽好了。絕對不准再踏進我家一步！懂了嗎？

🅑 (Go away angrily.)

(生氣地走開。)

情境對話2：

🅐 I can't hear you. It's too loud here.

我聽不見你。這裡太吵了。

🅑 Read my lips. I said "Don't forget to return my novel to the library tomorrow."

讀我的唇。我說"明天不要忘記把我的書還給圖書館。"

字　彙

lip 嘴唇　　　　　　　　step 踏進

angrily 生氣地　　　　　novel 小說

180. Right now!

就是現在！

說　明

此句等於 Right away./Immediately.加上 right 是更強調語氣。當你希望對方能處理一件你覺得應立即解決的事時，就可以用這句話，但此句帶有命令的意味，所以通常用在上位者對下位者的情境中。

情境對話1：

Ⓐ Right now! Catch the ball!

就是現在！接住球！

Ⓑ Yes, I caught it!

太好了，我接到了！

情境對話2：

Ⓐ Sir, when will you announce the news?

長官，你什麼時候要宣布這消息？

Ⓑ Right now!

就是現在！

字　彙

catch 接；抓　　　　　　announce 宣布

181. See you.

再見。

說　明

此句等同於 Goodbye./Bye-bye.即與友人道別時，就可用這句話。

情境對話1：

Ⓐ It's time to say goodbye again.
又到了說再見的時候了。

Ⓑ Yes, it is. Then, see you next time.
是啊。那麼，下次再見了。

情境對話2：

Ⓐ See you, my dear friend.
再見了，我親愛的朋友。

Ⓑ Bye, Roy. I will call you when I reach New York.
再見了，羅伊。我到了紐約後會打給你的。

字　彙

reach 抵達；伸出　　　　New York 紐約

182. Seeing is believing.

眼見為憑。

說　明

　此句為常見之英語諺語，意即親眼看到某事時才始相信他人所說之事。因此，當你聽到他人所陳述之事情讓你無法相信或懷疑時，就可以用此句告訴他。

情境對話1：

Ⓐ Did you know that it was Tim that stole Jessica's purse?
你知道就是提姆偷了潔西卡的錢包嗎？

Ⓑ Seeing is believing. I need to see real evidence.
眼見為憑。我必須看到真確的證據。

情境對話2：

Ⓐ Seeing is believing ; thus, we can't judge anything without facts.
眼見為憑；因此我們不能沒有拿出事實就判斷任何事情。

Ⓑ Yes, it's true.
沒錯，的確如此。

字　彙

stole(steal 的過去式)偷竊　　evidence 證據
judge 判斷

183. She has a long face.

她的臉很臭。

說　明

當你看見某人的表情不是很好，像拉長臉似的時候，可能是因為心情不好所致時，就可以用這句話形容對方。

情境對話1：

Ⓐ What's wrong with Terry? She has a long face.
泰瑞怎麼了？她的臉很臭。

Ⓑ Well, because she just got scolded by her boss yesterday.
唉，因為她昨天被老闆罵了一頓。

情境對話2：

Ⓐ She has a long face, so you'd better leave her alone.
她的臉很臭，所以你最好離她遠一點。

Ⓑ Thank you for telling me this.
謝謝你告訴我。

字 彙
scold 責罵

---

184. Slow down.

慢一點。

說 明

　當你希望對方的速度慢一點時，不管是開車、說話或走路等等，就可以用這句話告訴對方，請他慢一點。

情境對話1：

Ⓐ Slow down, Allen. It's so dangerous for you to cross the street without looking around for cars.
慢一點，艾倫。你沒有看車子就直接穿越馬路是很危險的。

Ⓑ Ok. I know it now.
好的。我現在知道了。

情境對話2：

Ⓐ I couldn't catch what you said. Would you please slow down?
我不懂你所說的話。你可以說慢一點嗎？

Ⓑ Sorry, I would repeat it.
對不起，我再重複一次。

字 彙

cross 橫過　　　　　　street 街道
around 環顧(繞)　　　repeat 重複

185. So do I.

我也是。

說　明

當別人所敘述的事情或意見，讓你也有相同感受時，就可以用這句話回應。

情境對話 1：

Ⓐ What do you want to be when you grow up?
你長大後想當什麼？

Ⓑ I want to be a doctor so that I can rescue more people.
我想當醫生這樣子就可以拯救更多人。

Ⓐ So do I.
我也是。

情境對話 2：

Ⓐ I would like to experience the life of being a backpacker.
我想體驗背包客的生活。

Ⓑ So do I.
我也是

字　彙

experience 體驗　　　　　　　backpacker 背包客

186. So far so good.

目前為止一切都還好。

說　明

通常此句是對方用來詢問你的近況時所說的話，若你目前所進行的事情或生活情況都還不錯，沒有什麼突發意外時，就可以用這句話來回應。

情境對話1：

Ⓐ Carol, how's the progress of your doctoral thesis?
凱若，你的博士論文進度如何？

Ⓑ So far so good.
目前為止一切都還好。

情境對話2：

Ⓐ What do you think about the preparations for Mandy's wedding ceremony?
你覺得曼蒂的婚禮準備的如何？

Ⓑ So far so good. I think it will go smoothly.
目前為止一切都還好。我想婚禮應該會很順利地進行。

字 彙

progress 進度　　　　　　　doctoral 博士的
thesis 論文

---

187. Sorry to interrupt you.

抱歉打擾你。

說 明

　當你不小心打擾他人時，或是你有事要找對方，但對方正在忙時，就可以用上這句話。

情境對話1：

Ⓐ Sorry to interrupt you, but there is an emergency.
抱歉打擾你，但現在有一個緊急情況。

Ⓑ What happened?
怎麼了？

情境對話2：

Ⓐ Sorry to interrupt you. I didn't know you were in council now. I'll leave now.

抱歉打擾你。我不知道你在開會中。我馬上離開。

字　彙

emergency 緊急情況(事件)　　council 議事；會議

188. Suit yourself.

隨便你。

說　明

　　此句通常用於友人來家裡作客時，就可以用這句話告訴對方，以示可以把這裡當作自己家一樣，要喝水或上廁所等一些小事，就自己來的意思。但也可以用在平常一般事情上的決定，例如對方想做某件事而詢問你的看法時，而你認為對方可自行決定，沒有意見時，就可以用這句話回應。

情境對話1：

Ⓐ Excuse me. May I use the bathroom?

不好意思。我可以借用廁所嗎？

Ⓑ Yeah, suit yourself.

可以呀，隨便你。

情境對話2：

Ⓐ Emma, what's your suggestion about the report?

艾瑪，關於這份報告你有什麼建議嗎？

Ⓑ I don't have any opinion. Just suit yourself.

我沒有任何意見。隨你決定。

字　彙

suggestion 建議

189. Take a look.

看一下。

說　明

當你希望對方可以看一下你所要呈現或指定的東西時，就可以用上這句話。

情境對話1：

Ⓐ Take a look. Does this T-shirt suit me?
看一下。這件 T 恤適合我嗎？

Ⓑ Not bad. It looks good on you.
不錯。你穿起來好看。

情境對話2：

Ⓐ Vincent, take a look at the financial report.
文森，看一下這份財務報告。

Ⓑ Oh, no. We are in the red this month.
喔，不。我們這個月呈現虧損。

字　彙

T-shirt T 恤　　　　　　　　financial 財政的；金融的
in the red 虧損

190. Take care.

保重。

說　明

當你的朋友或家人要離開或遠行時，就可以用上這句話。希望對方一路上小心、保重好自己。

情境對話1：

Ⓐ I'm going to take the flight to Peru tomorrow.
我明天將要搭機前往秘魯。

Ⓑ Take care and hope to see you soon again.
保重並希望能儘快再見到你。

情境對話2：

Ⓐ Take care, my children.
保重了，孩子們。

Ⓑ So do you, mom. We will come back home in a month.
你也是，媽。我們一個月之後就會回來了。

字　彙

flight 航程　　　　　　　Peru 祕魯

191. Thanks a lot.

多謝。

說　明

此句等於 Thank you very much.當別人有恩或有助於你時，就可以用此句回應。

情境對話1：

Ⓐ Could you please help me buy a vacuum bottle? Mine was broken last week.
可以請你幫我買一個保溫瓶嗎？我的上星期壞掉了。

Ⓑ Sure.
當然。

Ⓐ Thanks a lot!
多謝啦！

情境對話2：

Ⓐ Thanks a lot for giving me such a precious necklace.
謝謝你送我這麼珍貴的項鍊。

Ⓑ You deserve it.
這是你應該得到的。

字　彙

vacuum　真空	bottle　瓶子
precious　珍貴的	necklace　項鍊
deserve　應得	

192. That's all I need.

我就要這些。

說　明

　　當對方提供你所需要的資訊或東西時，而你只要這些或其中某部分時，就可以用此句回答他。

情境對話1：

Ⓐ Here is the file you need.
你要的檔案在這裡。

Ⓑ Thank you. That's all I need.
謝謝你。我就要這些。

情境對話2：

Ⓐ Ok. That's all I need. This one and that one.
好。我要的就是這些。這一個和那一個。

Ⓑ How about others?
那其他的呢？

字　彙

others　其他

193. That's it.

夠了。/就是這樣了。

說　明

此句之意會因對話情境而有差異。當你受不了對方或事情(例，工作、家庭、感情⋯⋯等等)所給你的壓力時，就可以用此句表示"夠了"。或者，當你對於某件事情的看法或其發展狀況認為"就是這樣了"，也可用此句表達。

情境對話1：

Ⓐ How could you just leave me alone when I felt upset last night? And why didn't you answer my phone?

你昨晚怎麼可以在我難過時留我一人呢？而且你為什麼不回我的電話呢？

Ⓑ That's it! I don't want to talk about that.

夠了！我不想談這件事。

情境對話2：

Ⓐ Is there anything else you need? Sir?

先生，你還需要什麼嗎？

Ⓑ No, that's it.

不，就是這樣了。

字　彙

night 夜晚

194. That's 3the stupidest thing I've ever heard!

那是我聽到的最愚蠢的事！

說　明

當你聽到一件你覺得很蠢的事情時，就可以用這句話表示。

情境對話1：

Ⓐ Did you hear what Danny just said?
你聽到剛剛丹尼所說的嗎？

Ⓑ Yeah. That's the stupidest thing I've ever heard!
有啊。那是我聽過最愚蠢的事了！

情境對話2：

Ⓐ That's the stupidest thing I've ever heard! Why would you do that?
那是我聽過最愚蠢的事了！你怎麼會做那件事呢？

Ⓑ Well, I was forced.
唉，我是被迫的。

字　彙

force 逼迫

195. That's your problem.

那是你的問題。

說　明

當你和對方起爭執時，明明錯不在自己身上時，而是對方，就可以用這句話表示。

情境對話1：

Ⓐ That's your problem.
那是你的問題。

Ⓑ How could you blame me? You are involved in it as well.
你怎麼可以怪我？你也有參與其中。

情境對話2：

Ⓐ Why did our daughter take a French leave?
為什麼我們的女兒不告而別？

Ⓑ That's your problem! Because she can't put up with your nagging her very day.
那是你的問題！因為她受不了你每天對她嘮叨。

字　彙

blame 責怪	involve 參與；涉入
French leave 不告而別	put up with 忍受
nag 嘮叨	

---

196. That makes no difference.

沒什麼差別。

說　明

當對方詢問你對於某幾件事物相較的看法時，若你覺得沒有什麼差別時，就可用此句做為回應。另外，當某事物對你或對某人、某事物不會造成嚴重的影響，或讓你覺得無所謂時，也可以用這句話。

情境對話1：

Ⓐ That makes no difference for me to wear this white suit or that black suit.
對我來說穿這件白色西裝或那件黑色西裝，沒有什麼差別。

B But it matters to me, especially at my grandmother's birthday party.
但對我而言很重要，特別是在我祖母的慶生會上。

情境對話2：

A What do you think about raising a dog or a cat?
你覺得養狗好還是養貓好？

B Well, that makes no difference!
那沒什麼差別吧！

字　彙

difference 差異　　　　　raise 飼養；舉起

---

197. The answer is zero.

白忙了。

說　明

　當你所進行的計畫或是活動等，到頭來還是一場空時，就可以用這句話表示白忙了。

情境對話1：

A No matter how hard I try, the answer is zero eventually.
無論我多努力嘗試，最終還是白忙了。

B Don't give up easily. Let's figure it out again.
別輕易放棄。我們再一起想辦法解決。

情境對話2：

A Hey, Josh. How's your research?
嘿，喬許。你的研究如何？

B The answer is zero.
一切都白忙了。

字　彙

zero 零　　　　　　　　　　easily 輕易地

figure out 想出；理解

198. The price is reasonable.

價格還算合理。

說　明

當你覺得某物品的價格合理時，就可以用上這句話。

情境對話1：

Ⓐ How much does the tuxedo cost?
這套燕尾服要價多少？

Ⓑ It costs 7,500 dollars. But I think the price is reasonable.
七千五百元。但我認為價格還算合理。

情境對話2：

Ⓐ The price of the meal in this Italian restaurant is reasonable.
這家義大利餐廳的餐點價位還算合理。

Ⓑ Yeah, except the dessert.
是啊，除了甜點以外。

字　彙

tuxedo 燕尾服(晚禮服)

reasonable 合理的；通情達理的

meal 餐點

Italian 義大利的

except 除~以外

dessert 甜點

199. Things are getting better.

情況正在好轉。

說　明

當某事進行的情況或身體的狀況由壞轉好，或是從毫無起色到漸漸變好時，就可以用上這句話。

情境對話1：

🅐 How's the situation of Jane's recovery?
珍復原的情況如何？

🅑 Things are getting better.
情況正在好轉。

情境對話2：

🅐 Things are getting better since your participating in this company.
自從你加入這間公司後情況有好轉。

🅑 Really? I'm flattered.
真的嗎？你過獎了。

字　彙

situation 情況	recovery 復原
since 自從	participate 參與
flatter 諂媚；奉承	

200. Think twice.　(099)

三思而後行。

說　明

當你希望對方在下決定做某件事之前，能再三考慮時，就可以用這句話告訴他。

情境對話1：

Ⓐ I made up my mind to buy this mansion.
我決定要買下這棟大樓。

Ⓑ You need to think twice for it will cost you a large amount of money.
你需要三思而後行，因為這會花掉你一大筆錢。

情境對話2：

Ⓐ Jason, please think twice before you make any decision. Ok?
傑森，下任何決定前請三思而後行，好嗎？

Ⓑ Ok, I know. I'll keep that in my mind.
好的，我知道了。我會謹記在心。

字　彙

make up one's mind 決定　　　　mansion 大樓；大廈

a large amount 大量；許多

201. **This way.**

往這邊。

說　明

當你跟對方說往這個方向走時，就可以用此句表達。

情境對話1：

Ⓐ Could you show me where the conference room is?
你可以告訴我會議室怎麼走嗎？

Ⓑ Sure. This way.
當然。往這邊走。

情境對話2：

Ⓐ This way. Do you see the drugstore?
往這邊走。你看見那間藥局了嗎？

Ⓑ Yes, thank you anyway.
我看到了，謝謝你喔！

字　彙

drugstore 藥局

---

202. Time flies.

時光飛逝。

說　明

　　若想跟對方表示要珍惜時間，就可以用上這句話，使對方知道要把握時間。另外，當你從事某件事情或活動時，非常投入其中，然後停止該事情或活動時，才發現時間已超過自己所認為的時間時，也可以用此句表示。

情境對話1：

Ⓐ Time flies and I still get stuck at this issue.
時間飛逝而我仍卡在這個問題上。

Ⓑ Do you need any help?
你需要幫忙嗎？

情境對話2：

Ⓐ What time is it now?
現在幾點了？

Ⓑ It's almost midnight!
要近半夜囉！

Ⓐ Gosh! Time flies.
天哪！時間過得真快。

字　彙

stuck 困住　　　　　　　　midnight 半夜

---

203. **Time is money.**

時間就是金錢。

說　明

此句所欲表示之意思類似 **Time flies.** 但此句更強調時間的價值性，所以有時候為了省時間，有些人會用金錢來縮短原本所預定的時間，此時就可以用此句表達。

情境對話1：

🅐 Since time is money. I decide to do things efficiently from now on.

既然時間就是金錢，那我決定從現在起要有效率的做事情。

🅑 Good. Hope you can really fulfill what you say.

很好。希望你能做到你說的。

情境對話2：

🅐 Time is money so we should hire more workers.

時間就是金錢，所以我們應該僱用更多的工人。

🅑 I agree, too.

我也贊成。

字　彙

efficiently 有效率地

from now on 從現在起

fulfill 實踐

hire 僱用

204. **Time's up!**

(101)

> 時間到！

說　明

　　此句常用於一項活動、考試或比賽進行的情況下，當時間一到所指定的時間時，就可以用此句表示。

情境對話1：

Ⓐ Time's up! Stop.
　　時間到！停。

情境對話2：

Ⓐ If time's up, will you stay with me?
　　如果時間到了，你會和我待在一起嗎？

Ⓑ Yes, I will. I promise I will be right here with you even if the sky collapses.
　　會，我會的。我保證我會在這裡陪著你，即使天塌下來。

字　彙

even if 即使　　　　　　　　　collapse 倒塌

205. **To go.**

> 外帶

說　明

　　若不想在餐廳內用餐，而改外帶時，就可用上此句。

情境對話1：

Ⓐ Sir, do you want to eat here or to go?
　　先生，你要內用還是外帶？

Ⓑ To go, please.
外帶，謝謝。

情境對話2：

Ⓐ I want a combo number 2 to go.
我要外帶一份2號餐。

Ⓑ Ok. Please wait here.
好的。請在這裡稍等一下。

字 彙

combo 套餐；結合物

---

206. Try again.

再試一次。

說 明

此句可用來鼓勵對方因考試、比賽、工作或任何事情、任務等受挫時所說的話。

情境對話1：

Ⓐ I couldn't reach the criterion my boss set.
我無法達成我老闆所設的標準。

Ⓑ Then try again!
那就再試一次！

情境對話2：

Ⓐ Let's try again to open the door.
我們再試一次把門打開。

Ⓑ No, we can't. The door is locked.
不，我們打不開的。門是鎖住的。

字　彙

criterion 標準　　　　　　　　set 設定

lock 上鎖

207. Turn on the light.

開燈。

說　明

　　此句常用於家中或工作場所中，或是到任一燈光昏暗或沒有燈光之處，就可以用上此句話。反之，則是關燈 Turn off the light. 這裡的 light 加不加 s 皆可；加上 the 則是表示特定地方的燈。

情境對話1：

A It's too dark here. I can hardly see anything.
這裡太暗了。我看不見東西。

B Why don't you turn on the light?
為什麼你不開燈？

情境對話2：

A Jamie, would you please help me turn on the light in the basement?
潔米，你可以幫我打開地下室的燈嗎？

B Sure. Wait a minute.
當然可以。等一下。

字　彙

basement 地下室

208. Turn right.

(103)

右轉。

說　明

　此句常用於問路或駕駛、乘坐交通工具時，若欲向對方表達右轉時，就可以用此句話。反之，則是 Turn left.

情境對話1：

Ⓐ Excuse me. Do you know how to go to the Taipei City Hall?

不好意思，請問一下。你知道怎麼到台北市政府嗎？

Ⓑ Yes. Start walking straight from here for two blocks and turn right.

知道。從這裡直走經過兩個街區後再右轉。

情境對話2：

Ⓐ You should turn right now.

你應該現在就要右轉。

Ⓑ You don't have to tell me that. I know how to get there.

你不用告訴我怎麼走。我知道怎麼到那裡。

字　彙

hall 會堂；大廳　　　　　block 街區；擋住

209. Wait a minute.

等一下！

說　明

　當你因為有事而希望對方等你，而不會花很久的時間時，就可以用此句話。此句等於 Wait a second/moment.或是 Just a moment.

情境對話1：

Ⓐ Wait a minute, Kate. I'll go to get my coat.
凱特，等一下。我去拿我的外套。

Ⓑ Ok. I'll wait here.
好。那我在這裡等。

情境對話2：

Ⓐ Wait a minute. What's going on?
等一下。發生什麼事？

Ⓑ Look! There is a man standing on the roof.
看！有一個人站在屋頂上。

字 彙

roof 屋頂

---

210. Wake up! (104)

醒來！/起床！

說 明

欲叫對方起床時，就可以用這句話。另外，當你發現對方發呆而沒有聽你講話時，或是過於沉迷、投入某些不切實際的情境時，也可用此句話喚醒對方，讓對方知道不要再作夢，要面對實際生活等之類的意思。

情境對話1：

Ⓐ Wake up, Wesley!
衛斯理，起床了！

Ⓑ No. I need more sleep.
不。我還想再睡。

情境對話2：

Ⓐ If I were the millionaire's son, I wouldn't have to worry about the rest of my life.
如果我是百萬富翁的兒子，我就不用擔憂我的餘生。

Ⓑ Wake up! It's impossible.
醒醒吧！那是不可能的。

字 彙

millionaire 百萬富翁

---

211. **Whatever.**

無所謂。

說 明

　這是年輕人很常用的俚語，除了無所謂外，還有"我不在乎！"以及"等等，諸如此類的"，或是"才不是那樣的，不過我才不理它。"的意思。所以這句話所代表的意思須視上下文而定。

情境對話1：

Ⓐ You can do what you want. Whatever.
你可以做任何你想做的。我無所謂。

Ⓑ Really?
真的嗎？

情境對話2：

Ⓐ He will carry on this task whatever the difficulties he may confront.
無論他遇到什麼難題，他仍會繼續這項任務。

Ⓑ I'm glad to hear what you say. Then I can trust him now.
我很高興聽到你這麼說。那麼，我現在可以相信他了。

每日一句 生活英語
Everyday English

字 彙

confront 面臨；遭遇　　　　trust 相信

---

212. What a nice day it is! 🎧 105

今天天氣真好!

說 明

　此句可用來當作打招呼或作為欲與對方開始談話的起頭，但前提是當時的天氣得真的是好天氣。

情境對話1：

A What a nice day it is.
今天天氣真好!

B Yeah! It seems a good day to go swimming.
是啊！看起來是個適合游泳的好天氣。

情境對話2：

A What a nice day it is!
今天天氣真好!

B Yes, it is. But, unfortunately I got bitten by a fierce dog on my way home.
沒錯。但不幸的是，我在回家的路上被一隻惡犬給咬了。

字 彙

unfortunately 不幸地
bitten(bite 的過去分詞)咬
fierce 兇猛的

213. Yes, I see.

是的，我懂了。

說　明

當你瞭解對方所表達的意思時，就可用此句話回應。

情境對話1：

🅐 Do you understand the article I mentioned to you last time?
你了解我上次跟你提過的那篇文章嗎？

🅑 Yes, I see.
懂，我懂。

情境對話2：

🅐 Yes, I see. So let's get started.
是的，我了解了。那我們開始吧。

🅑 Wait. I need to check it again to make sure.
等等。我需要再次檢查確認。

字　彙

article 文章　　　　　　　　mention 提及；說到

214. You are a chicken.

106

你是個膽小鬼。

說　明

當你覺得對方在某些方面，例如個性、與人相處上或處理一些事情時，表現出膽小畏怯時，就可以用這句話。但是，此句通常會用於熟識的人身上，尤其是同輩或晚輩。

情境對話1：

Ⓐ Don't tell me the ghost story for I'm afraid that I can't fall asleep.
別跟我講鬼故事，因為我怕我會睡不著。

Ⓑ You are a chicken. Actually, most of them are not real.
你真是個膽小鬼。其實大部分的鬼故事都不是真的。

情境對話2：

Ⓐ You are a chicken! It's just a cockroach.
你真膽小。牠只是一隻蟑螂而已。

字　彙

ghost 鬼	asleep 睡著的
actually 實際上	cockroach 蟑螂

215. You are just in time.

你來得正是時候。

說　明

當你欲跟對方表示你來的正是時候時，就可用這句話。而 in time 本意為及時，on time 則是準時。

情境對話1：

Ⓐ You are just in time, Daniel. The train is leaving now.
丹尼爾，你來得正是時候。火車正要開走了。

Ⓑ Ok, see you then!
好，再見了！

情境對話2：

Ⓐ Am I late for Bruce's commencement?
我遲了布魯斯的畢業典禮嗎？

B No, you are just in time.
不，你來得正是時候。

字　彙

commencement 畢業典禮

---

216. You asked for it.

這是你自找的。

說　明

當你欲跟對方表示此事情的結果(通常是負面的，或是麻煩)，是對方自己造成時，就可以用這句話表示。而且此句會帶有責備及生氣的意味。

情境對話1：

A You asked for it. Now, you missed Nick's bachelor party.
這是你自找的。現在可好了，你錯過了尼克的告別單身派對。

B But I was occupied with lots of business in the company last night.
但昨晚我忙著處理公司裡的一堆公事。

情境對話2：

A Oh, no! Professor Wells flunked me!
喔，不！威爾斯教授當了我！

B You asked for it. I had told you not to skip his class.
這是你自找的。我早就告訴過你不要翹他的課。

字　彙

bachelor 單身漢

flunk 使~不及格

skip class 翹課

217. **You're all alike.**

你們都是一丘之貉。/你們是同一夥的。

說　明

當你欲跟對方表示你們都是一個樣時(通常指不好的地方，例如：品行不良或是個性上的缺點、工作態度不佳、處理方式欠缺等)，就可用此句帶有責備和生氣意味的話表示。

情境對話1：

Ⓐ Look at what you've done! You're all alike!
你看你做的！你們都是一個樣！

情境對話2：

Ⓐ No wonder you and Mark are all alike. Both of you get into trouble every day.
難怪你和馬克是一夥的。你們兩個每天都惹麻煩。

Ⓑ It's not all our fault. Kevin also gets involved.
這又不全是我們的錯。凱文也有份。

字　彙

get into trouble　惹麻煩

218. **You're so careless.** 108

你真粗心。

說　明

當你認為對方所做的事情是因為對方粗心所致，而沒有使結果更臻於完善時，就可用這句話表示。例如：考試錯了不該錯的題目；打字打錯；公事上出了紕漏等等之類的過失(沒有造成很嚴重的負面結果)。

情境對話1：

Ⓐ Why didn't you read the questions carefully? You're so careless.
你為什麼不仔細看題目？你真是粗心。

Ⓑ Because the time was running out.
因為時間不夠了。

情境對話2：

Ⓐ Oops! I forgot to turn off the gas and air the bedcover.
噢！我忘了關瓦斯還有晾床單。

Ⓑ You're so careless. Now, you should hurry home.
你真粗心。現在你趕快回家吧。

字　彙

run out 用完；耗盡　　　　　gas 瓦斯

bedcover 床單

219. You can call me any time.

你可以隨時打電話給我。

說　明

當你認為對方需要幫忙時，就可以用此句表示你願意給予對方協助。

情境對話1：

Ⓐ If you need someone to assist you with the assignment, you can call me any time.
如果你需要人協助這項工作，你可以隨時打電話給我。

Ⓑ Thanks for your kindness.
謝謝你的好意。

情境對話 2：

Ⓐ I feel so depressed and disappointed.
我覺得好沮喪又失望。

Ⓑ You can call me any time, Annie.
安妮，你可以隨時打電話給我。

字　彙

assist 協助	depressed 沮喪的
disappointed 失望的	

---

220. You've got to do something.

你必須想個法子。

說　明

　當情況緊急時，而需要有人想辦法解決時，但自己又無能為力時，就可以用此句話向對方尋求協助。例如，自己的家人染上重病或絕症時，就可以用這句話跟醫生表示。

情境對話 1：

Ⓐ You've got to do something. The bomb is going to explode in ten minutes!
你必須想個法子。炸彈十分鐘內就會爆炸了！

Ⓑ I know! I am thinking!
我知道！我正在想呀！

情境對話 2：

Ⓐ Nina hasn't eaten any food for three days.
妮娜已經三天未進食了。

Ⓑ You've got to do something. She is your daughter!
你必須想個法子。她是你的女兒！

字 彙

bomb 炸彈　　　　　　　　　explode 爆炸

221. You need to see a doctor.

你該去看醫生。

說 明

　當你的親人、朋友或同事感冒生病時，或是身心狀況有出問題時，就可以用這句話告訴對方，請對方去就醫治療。

情境對話 1：

Ⓐ My body has been in pain for a week.
我的身體已經痛了一星期。

Ⓑ You need to see a doctor to do a physical check-up.
你需要看醫生做個體檢。

情境對話 2：

Ⓐ My back is so painful that I can't stand upright anymore.
我的背痛到讓我站不直。

Ⓑ Then, you need to see a doctor.
那你應該去看醫生。

字 彙

in pain 痛苦

physical 身體的

back 背部

painful 痛(苦)的

upright 挺直的

222. You need a workout. ⌢110

你需要去運動鍛鍊一下。

說　明

　　當你認為你的朋友、親人或熟識的人身體過於肥胖，或是需要靠運動來改善身心的情況時，就可以用上此句話。

情境對話1：

Ⓐ Oh, my god! My weight is 65 kilograms.
喔，我的天哪！我的體重是65公斤。

Ⓑ Well, you need a workout.
你需要去運動鍛鍊一下囉。

情境對話2：

Ⓐ You need a workout if your BMI is above the criteria range.
如果你的身體質量指數超過標準範圍，你就需要去運動了。

Ⓑ Yes, coach. I'll watch out for it.
是的，教練。我會注意的。

字　彙

weight 體重；重量
kilogram 公斤
workout 訓練
BMI(Body Mass Index)身體質量指數
above 在~以上
criteria(criterion 的複數)標準
coach 教練

223. **You never change.**

江山易改，本性難移。

說　明

　當你怎麼勸說你的友人應該改善自己的個性或待人處世的方式，但他卻不聽、成效不彰或根本改不了時，就可以用上此句話。

情境對話1：

Ⓐ You never change.
你真是本性難移。

Ⓑ Why do you say that?
為什麼這麼說？

Ⓐ Because after five years, you're still so stingy.
因為即使過了五年，你還是那麼小氣。

情境對話2：

Ⓐ You never change. You still ask me to buy you lunch every day.
你真是江山易改，本性難移。你還是每天要我買午餐給你。

Ⓑ But you do it all the time, so why can't I?
但你也常常這麼做，那為什麼我就不行？

字　彙

stingy 小氣；吝嗇

224. **You owe me one.**

你欠我一個人情。

說　明

　　當你幫了對方一個忙，也希望對方記住或改天回饋你時，就可以用這句話表示。但並非真的命令對方就一定要還自己一個人情，必須視說話者所表達的意願或語氣而定。

情境對話1：

Ⓐ Do you remember that you owe me one?
你記得你欠我一個人情嗎？

Ⓑ When? And what is it?
什麼時候？欠你什麼啊？

情境對話2：

Ⓐ Cassie, could you substitute my English class only for tomorrow, please?
凱西，可以請你幫我代明天的英文課嗎？

Ⓑ Again. You owe me one.
又來了。你欠我一個人情。

字　彙

substitute 代課

Chapter 3

表達身心情緒狀態用語

225. Cut it out. 111

省省吧。/停止，別鬧了。

說　明

當你的家人、朋友或同事中，有人一直互相爭來吵去，或是重複同樣的話、抱怨等之類的，讓你受不了時，就可以用這句話告訴他們停止別再吵，或是別再抱怨了。另外，要注意的是，**Cut it out!** 中間的 **it** 是不可用其他代名詞取代的。

情境對話1：

Ⓐ My back is aching, and my ... I'm aching all over.
我的背好痛，我的......，我的全身都在痛。

Ⓑ Cut it out! I told you to see a doctor, but you didn't listen.
夠了！我叫你去看醫生，但你卻不聽。

情境對話2：

Ⓐ Stop fighting, you two! Cut it out!
你們兩個別吵了！停止，別再鬧了！

Ⓑ But Harry started it first!
可是是哈利先開始的！

字　彙

ache 疼痛

226. Don't be that way!

別那樣！

說　明

當你的朋友、家人或同事做出或說出讓你覺得不恰當或不理智的言行舉止時，就可以用這句話勸阻他們，先讓他們冷靜下來，然後再聽你解釋或規勸。

情境對話 1：

🅐 Don't be that way. If you don't obey the instructions, you might get hurt.

別那樣做！如果你不依指示，你可能會受傷。

🅑 Don't worry. It's not that serious.

別擔心。又沒那麼嚴重。

情境對話 2：

🅐 I really want to move out right now. I can't stand those selfish roommates anymore.

我真想現在就搬出去。我再也受不了那些自私的室友了。

🅑 Please don't be that way. Calm down.

請別那樣！冷靜一下。

字　彙

obey 遵守	selfish 自私的
roommate 室友	calm 冷靜

227. Don't bother me!　🎧112

別煩我！

說　明

當你在忙碌，或想一個人靜一靜時，卻有人打擾你，讓你受不了甚至感到生氣，就可以用這句話告訴對方。

情境對話 1：

🅐 Hey, Dan. Do you have time now? I need your assistance with this DVD player.

嘿，丹。你現在有空嗎？我需要你幫我弄一下這個 DVD 播放器。

B Please don't bother me now. I have an important test tomorrow.

現在請不要煩我。我明天有個重要的考試。

情境對話2：

A Don't bother me!

別煩我！

B Sorry. But it won't take you much time.

對不起。但這不會花你太多時間的。

字　彙

player　播放器

---

228. Don't give me that!

少來這套!

說　明

當你識破對方使用藉口或是 "好聽、合理" 的話的真正意圖時，就可以用這句話表示。

情境對話1：

A Don't give me that! I'm sick of your excuses for being late.

少來這套！我已經受夠你那些遲到的理由了。

B But I was really stuck in a traffic jam this time.

但我這次是真的塞車。

情境對話2：

A Mom, can I go out with my friends?

媽，我可以和我的朋友出去嗎？

B Don't give me that! You just want to sneak out to have some fun with your fair-weather friends.

少來這套！你只是想和你的酒肉朋友們出去找樂子而已。

字 彙

traffic jam 塞車　　　　　　　sneak 偷溜

fair-weather friend 不能共患難的朋友

---

229. Don't go too far.

別太過分。

說 明

當對方所說的話或是表示的動作讓人覺得超過常理，或是感覺不舒服，有逾越的言行時，就可以用此句表示。

情境對話1：

A I definitely will not admit he belongs to a part of us.

我絕對不承認他是我們的一份子。

B Don't go too far, Ryan. At least, he is one of our family members.

萊恩，別太過分。至少，他是我們的家人。

情境對話2：

A Don't go too far, Max! This is not your territory.

麥克斯，別太過分！這不是你的地盤。

B Oh, really? I'll show you who the boss is here.

喔，真的嗎？我會讓你知道誰是這裡的老大。

字 彙

admit 承認　　　　　　　belong 屬於

territory 領域

230. Don't nag me!

別對我碎碎唸！

說　明

當對方(通常是熟識的家人或朋友)一直對你重複說同樣的話或抱怨你哪裡做不好、哪裡要改進等，讓你覺得很煩時，就可以用這句話。

情境對話1：

Ⓐ Please don't nag me. It will make me feel annoyed.
請別對我碎碎唸。那只會讓我覺得很煩。

Ⓑ But it's for your own good.
但這是為了你好。

情境對話2：

Ⓐ Why do you always forget to turn off the light when you leave your bedroom? And why do you⋯⋯
為什麼你離開臥室時總是忘了關燈？而且你為什麼⋯⋯？

Ⓑ Don't nag me again, Mom. I am tired now!
媽，別再對我碎碎唸了！我現在很累！

字　彙

annoyed 惱怒、氣惱的　　　　for one's own good 為了～好

231. Don't talk to me like that!

別那樣和我說話！

說　明

當你覺得對方講話的語氣惹惱你或讓你覺得很討厭或不舒服、不受尊重時，好像他是你的誰時，就可以用這句話回應他。

情境對話1：

Ⓐ Don't talk to me like that! You're not my mom.
別那樣和我說話！你又不是我媽。

Ⓑ If I were your mom, I would kick you out of my home.
如果我是你媽，我會把你踢出家門。

情境對話2：

Ⓐ You are not supposed to cohabit with your boyfriend.
你不該和你男友同居。

Ⓑ Don't talk to me like that. Who do you think you are?
別那樣和我說話！你以為你是誰？

字　彙

supposed to 應該；可以　　　cohabit 同居

232. **Don't touch me!**

別碰我！

說　明

　無論何時，當你不希望別人觸碰你時，就可以用此句表示。另外，這裡的 me 可以改成任何你不希望別人所觸碰的東西，例:Don't touch my book.(不要碰我的書。)加上 please，則是較委婉的拒絕方式。

情境對話1：

Ⓐ Don't touch me. I'm exhausted now.
別碰我。我現在非常累。

情境對話2：

Ⓐ The oven is out of order. So don't touch it temporarily.
這台烤箱故障了。所以暫時不要碰它。

Ⓑ But, it needs repairing.
但是，它需要送修。

字　彙

oven 烤箱	out of order 故障
temporarily 暫時地	repair 修理

233. Get lost. 114

滾開！

說　明

當某人讓你很生氣，或是你心情極度不好或暴躁時，就可以用這句話跟對方說，表示你不想見到他或他們。但這句話接近責罵的口氣，語氣非常地重，吵架時常會用到這句話。

情境對話1：

Ⓐ Get lost! I don't want to see your face anymore.
滾開！我不想再看到你的臉。

Ⓑ Fine! As you wish. You'll never see me again!
好！就如你所願。你再也不會見到我！

情境對話2：

Ⓐ How could you break this cup? It matters a lot to me!
你怎麼可以弄破這個杯子？它對我很重要！

Ⓑ Get lost! Stop nagging! It's just a cup.
滾開！不要再碎碎念了！它只是個杯子而已。

字　彙

as 如同	nag 抱怨

234. **Get off my case.**

別管我。

說　明
　如果你不希望對方管你的事情，或是對方很嘮叨，或者干涉你的決定時，就可以用這句話。此句的語氣也是較強烈的。

情境對話1：
Ⓐ You never tidy your room. You're so lazy.
　你從不收拾自己的房間。你真懶惰。

Ⓑ Get off my case.
　別管我。

情境對話2：
Ⓐ Get off my case.
　別管我。

Ⓑ But you're thirty years old now. Grow up!
　但你現在已經三十歲了。成熟點吧！

字　彙
tidy 整理清潔　　　　　　　　lazy 懶惰的

235. **Get out of my face!**　115

從我面前消失！

說　明
　當你不想看到對方時，就可以用這句話。此句用法如同 Get lost!

情境對話1：
Ⓐ Get out of my face! You nasty man!
　從我面前消失！你這個討厭鬼！

B Who do you think you are? Why do I have to listen to you?

你以為你是誰？為什麼我要聽你的？

情境對話2：

A You idiot! You ruined my entire plan. Get out of my face right away!

你這個白癡！你壞了我整個計畫。馬上從我面前消失！

字 彙

nasty　下流的；討厭的　　　　　idiot　白癡；笨蛋

entire　完整的；全部的

236. Give me a break.

饒了我吧。

說 明

當對方對你提出不合理的要求或一直要你做某件事時，就可以用這句話表示求饒。

情境對話1：

A Zoe, can you lend me your car?

柔伊，你可以借我你的車嗎？

B Give me a break! Don't you remember that you broke my car last time?

饒了我吧！你不記得你上次弄壞了我的車嗎？

情境對話2：

A Give me a beak, mom! You can buy anything you want but except durian. I hate the smell.

饒了我吧，媽！你可以買任何你要的東西，除了榴槤以外。我討厭那味道。

Ⓑ But somehow I find it tastes good.
但不知為何我覺得它嘗起來不錯啊！

字　彙

durian 榴槤

somehow 由於某種未知的原因；不知怎麼的

---

237. How dare you!

你敢！

說　明

　當對方做出或說出讓你很驚訝，或讓你有受到冒犯之意時，就可以用這句話表示。

情境對話1：

Ⓐ How dare you ask me such a question?
你怎麼敢問我這樣的問題？

Ⓑ Sorry! If that embarrasses you, you don't have to answer.
對不起！如果這問題會為難你的話，你可以不用回答。

情境對話2：

Ⓐ Sherry, may I visit your room?
雪莉，我可以參觀你的房間嗎？

Ⓑ How dare you! We are not that close and you are not my boyfriend.
你敢！我們又沒那麼熟，而且你又不是我的男朋友。

字　彙

dare 膽敢　　　　　　　embarrass 使困窘、不安；尷尬

close 親近的；接近的

238. I'm all in.

我累到筋疲力竭。

說 明

此句等於 I'm exhausted./I'm very tired.指真的因為忙碌或處理事情到很疲累的狀態。

情境對話1：

Ⓐ I'm all in. I can't even move my finger.
我累到筋疲力竭。我累到甚至移一根手指頭都不行。

Ⓑ What made you so exhausted?
什麼事情讓你這麼累啊？

情境對話2：

Ⓐ What's wrong with you?
你怎麼了？

Ⓑ I'm all in after shopping with my three nephews for four hours.
在和我的三個外甥逛街逛了四個小時後，我累到筋疲力竭。

字 彙

nephew 姪兒；外甥

239. I'm all thumbs!

117

我真是笨手笨腳！

說 明

all thumbs用來形容對某件事情或領域不擅長時，就可以用此表示。例如：I'm all thumbs with dancing.（我不擅長跳舞。）或是做某件事情時，處理得不好，例如，端盤子端到掉下來，也可以用此句表示。

情境對話1：

Ⓐ I dropped my coffee cup. I'm all thumbs today.
我把咖啡杯掉在地上。我今天真是笨手笨腳。

Ⓑ It's ok. It's just a cup.
沒有關係。那只是一個杯子而已。

情境對話2：

Ⓐ Kevin, are you good at chemistry?
凱文，你化學好嗎？

Ⓑ No, I'm all thumbs with that.
不，我化學一竅不通。

字　彙

drop 掉落　　　　　　　　thumb 大拇指
chemistry 化學

240. I'm fed up with my work!

我受夠我這個工作了!

說　明

　此句中的 be fed up with 就是指 "受夠了" 的意思。也可用 be sick of/be tired of/can't tolerate/can't stand 等表示。with 後面的名詞可換成其他所受不了的事物。

情境對話1：

Ⓐ I'm fed up with my work!
我受夠我這個工作了！

Ⓑ Then, you should change another one.
那麼，你應該換個工作了。

情境對話2：

Ⓐ Why do you seem so angry?
為什麼你看起來很生氣？

Ⓑ I'm fed up with my work! My boss is strict and doesn't have the sense of responsibility.
我受夠我這個工作了!我的老闆嚴苛且沒有責任感。

字　彙

fed up　感到厭煩的；忍無可忍

strict　嚴苛的

241. I'm so sorry.

(118)

我很抱歉。

說　明

　當你做錯事情時，就可以用此句跟對方表示你的歉意。另外，sorry 也可解釋成遺憾。最常用於聽到對方所說的壞消息或有人去世時，就可用此句表示你的遺憾。

情境對話1：

Ⓐ I'm so sorry I hurt your feelings. But I didn't mean it.
我很抱歉我傷害了你的感情。但我不是故意的。

Ⓑ I've nothing to say. Just leave.
我已經沒有話好說了。你走吧。

情境對話2：

Ⓐ My uncle passed away one month ago.
我的叔叔一個月前過世。

Ⓑ I'm so sorry to hear that.
我很遺憾聽到這事。

字 彙
feeling 感情；感覺

242. I'm what I am.

我就是我。

說 明
當別人一直希望你改變你原來的樣子或個性時，就可以用這句話告訴他，表示你就是喜歡原本的自己，不要想改變我。

情境對話1：

A You should dye your hair brown which would make you look younger.
你應該把頭髮染成咖啡色，那會讓你看起來比較年輕點。

B I'm what I am. Thanks for your advice, but you can share it with others.
我就是我。謝謝你的建議，但你把它留給別人吧。

情境對話2：

A I'm what I am. No one can interfere with me or alter my decision.
我就是我。沒有人可以干涉我或是改變我的決定。

B You should learn to accept others' opinions.
你應該學習接受他人的意見。

字 彙
dye 染   interfere with 干涉
alter 改變

243. I can't take it anymore!
（119）

我受不了了！

說　明
當某件事或某個人讓你受不了時，就可以用此句表示。

情境對話1：

Ⓐ I can't take it anymore! I decide to study abroad.
我再也受不了了！我決定出國讀書。

Ⓑ Why?
為什麼？

情境對話2：

Ⓐ This view makes me so sad. I can't take it anymore.
這景象讓人太難過了。我再也受不了了。

Ⓑ Me, too. Let's go.
我也是。我們走吧。

字　彙

abroad 國外　　　　　　　　view 景象

244. I don't want to hear it!

我不想聽！

說　明
當對方說了一些讓你不想聽的話時，例如，數落自己的話，或是任何讓你生氣、難過的話，就可以用此句告訴他。

情境對話1：

Ⓐ Do you know how hard I raised you up? And now? Look what you've done!

你知道我多麼辛苦地把你養大嗎？而現在呢？你看你做了什麼！

Ⓑ I don't want to hear it!

我不想聽！

情境對話2：

Ⓐ I don't want to hear it! Please go away!

我不想聽！請你走開！

Ⓑ Ok, I'll let you calm down to think it over.

好，我會讓你冷靜下來好好想想。

字　彙

raise up 扶養　　　　　think over 仔細考慮

---

245. **I do.**

我願意。

說　明

　　此句最常用於答應求婚時，或在結婚進行時表示願意嫁給對方時所說的話。但也可以用在其他地方，表示我會這麼做，或是我瞭解的意思。因此，其意的解釋須視上下文而定。

情境對話1：

Ⓐ Would you marry me, Helen?

海倫，你願意嫁給我嗎？

Ⓑ Yes, I do.

是的，我願意。

情境對話2：

Ⓐ Do you think you are qualified to take this position?
你認為你能勝任這個職位嗎？

Ⓑ Yes, I do. I think I have enough confidence and competence for this job.
是的，我可以。我認為我有足夠的信心和能力接下這份工作。

字　彙

confidence 信心　　　　　　　　competence 能力

---

246. I got goose bumps.

我都起雞皮疙瘩了。

說　明

當你看到某個畫面或聽到某件事情、聲音時，會讓你起雞皮疙瘩時，就可用這句話表示。

情境對話1：

Ⓐ I got goose bumps all over my body.
我全身都起雞皮疙瘩了。

Ⓑ Why?
為什麼？

Ⓐ Because I heard the voice of scratching the blackboard.
因為我聽到刮黑板的聲音。

情境對話2：

Ⓐ Every time I see the insects and reptile animals, I get goose bumps.
每次我看到昆蟲和爬蟲類，我就會起雞皮疙瘩。

B So do I.
　我也是。

字　彙

goose 鵝	bump 碰撞
scratch 刮；擦	blackboard 黑板
insect 昆蟲	reptile 爬蟲類（的）

247. I hate you!　　　　　(121)

　　我討厭你！

說　明

　當你很討厭對方時，就可以用這句話表示。當然，此句的 you 可以改成任何所討厭的東西。

情境對話1：

A I hate you! You always attribute all the faults to me.
　我討厭你！你總是把所有的錯都怪到我身上。

情境對話2：

A I hate this photo. It reminds me of my unhappy child-hood.
　我討厭這張照片。它讓我想起我不快樂的童年。

B Give it to me. I'll throw that into the trash can.
　把它給我。我會把它丟到垃圾桶去。

字　彙

attribute 把～歸因(歸咎)於
childhood 童年時期
trash can 垃圾桶

248. I have a headache.

我頭痛。

說　明

當你的頭痛時就可以用此句表示。而此句中的 a 不可用 the 替代。

情境對話1：

A I don't feel well and I have a serious headache.
我身體不太舒服而且我的頭很痛。

B I think you'd better take a rest.
我想你最好去休息一下。

情境對話2：

A How do you feel now? Do you still have a headache?
你現在覺得如何？你頭還在痛嗎？

B I feel better now, but I still feel a little bit of dizzy.
我現在覺得好多了，但是我還是覺得有點頭暈。

字　彙

dizzy 暈的

249. I have a stomache.

我肚子痛。

說　明

當你肚子痛時，就可以用這句話表示。

情境對話1：

A You look so pale. What's wrong with you?
你臉色看起來很蒼白。你怎麼了？

Ⓑ I need to use the restroom. I have a stomache.
我需要上廁所。我肚子痛。

情境對話2：

Ⓐ Sorry, I can't continue the conversation with you. I have a stomache.
對不起，我現在無法和你對話。我肚子痛。

Ⓑ It's ok. Do you need to take some aspirin?
沒關係。你需要吃阿斯匹靈嗎？

字　彙

pale 蒼白的　　　　　　　　aspirin 阿斯匹靈

---

250. I have a toothache.

我牙齒痛。

說　明

當你牙齒痛的時候，就可以用這句表示。

情境對話1：

Ⓐ I have a toothache.
我牙齒痛。

Ⓑ Then, you need to see a dentist.
那麼，你需要去看牙醫。

情境對話2：

Ⓐ What happened to your face? It swells.
你的臉怎麼了？它腫起來了。

Ⓑ I have a toothache because of my wisdom tooth.
因為我的智齒讓我覺得牙齒很痛。

字　彙

dentist 牙醫　　　　　　swell 腫痛

wisdom 智慧

251. I've lost my appetite.　123

我沒食慾。

說　明

　當別人問你要不要吃東西，而你不想吃或因為沒有食慾時，就可以用這句話告訴對方。

情境對話1：

Ⓐ I've lost my appetite.
我沒有食慾。

Ⓑ Why?
為什麼？

Ⓐ I don't know, either. I just don't want to eat anything.
我也不知道。我就是不想吃東西。

情境對話2：

Ⓐ That food makes me feel like vomiting.
那食物讓我想吐。

Ⓑ Me, too. I've lost my appetite.
我也是。我沒有食慾了。

字　彙

appetite 胃口；食慾

feel like 想

vomit 嘔吐

252. I love you!

我愛你！

說　明

　當你想和對方表示愛意，就可以用這句話。此句常用於情侶、家人或交情深厚的朋友之間。

情境對話1：

Ⓐ I love you, mom. I swear I won't do things that will break your heart.
媽，我愛你。我發誓我不會做出讓你心碎的事情。

Ⓑ I'm glad to hear that.
我很高興聽到你這麼說。

情境對話2：

Ⓐ Why do you treat me so good and buy me lots of things I want?
為什麼你對我這麼好，而且買很多我想要的東西給我？

Ⓑ Because I love you.
因為我愛你。

字　彙

swear 發誓

253. It's incredible!

真是不可思議!

說　明

　當你看見或聽見某個讓你感到很驚訝或不可思議的畫面、事情時，就可以用這句話表示。或當你完成自己未預期的工作或是達成目標時，也可以用這句話表示。

情境對話 1：

A It's incredible that I completed this difficult worksheet!
我竟然完成了這張困難的練習卷，真是不可思議！

B Wow! You are really amazing!
哇！你真是太厲害了！

情境對話 2：

A Do you know that Clark successfully reached the summit of Mount Everest?
你知道克拉克成功地攻頂聖母峰嗎？

B No, I don't know that. But it's truly incredible!
不，我不知道。但這真的是不可思議！

字 彙

worksheet 工作單；練習卷　　summit 尖峰；峰頂
Mount Everest 聖母峰

---

254. It's amazing!

真是太令人驚訝了！

說 明

　此句類似 It's incredible!但此句更常用來形容看見某些很好、很棒或是令人讚嘆訝異的畫面。

情境對話 1：

A It's amazing! Look at the model's figure! It's so perfect and beautiful.
真是太令人驚訝了！你看那位模特兒的身材！真是完美又美麗。

B Yeah! It's very commonly seen in the show business.
是啊，沒錯！這在演藝圈裡很常見。

情境對話2：

Ⓐ I'd like to go to Nicaragua to view the spectacular scene of waterfall.
我想到尼加拉瓜去看那壯觀的瀑布景象。

Ⓑ I saw it last year. It's amazing!
我去年有看過。它真的太令人驚訝了！

字　彙

perfect 完美的	show business 演藝圈；娛樂圈
scene 景色	waterfall 瀑布

255. It surprised me. 　125

那事使我頗感驚訝。

說　明

某件事情(通常是指出乎意料之外的)讓你感到震驚時，就可用這句話表示，不論好或壞。

情境對話1：

Ⓐ It surprised me that when I learned that he was taking drugs.
當我得知他吸毒的消息時，真的讓我很吃驚。

Ⓑ So do I. I can't even believe it now.
我也是。我甚至到現在還無法相信。

情境對話2：

Ⓐ Keller was in prison for arson.
凱勒因為縱火而入獄。

Ⓑ Really? It really surprised me.
真的嗎？那真的是讓我吃驚。

字　彙

learn 得知；學習　　　　drug 藥品；毒品

prison 監獄　　　　　　arson 縱火(罪)

256. I'll never forgive you!

我永遠都不會原諒你！

說　明

　當對方做了某件讓你很憤怒、傷心或是不該做的事情時(通常是負面的事情)，就可以用這句話告訴對方，表示你真的很憤怒，且甚至有記仇或報復的傾向。而此句的受詞 you，可以改成任何對象。所以此句的語氣是非常的重，要注意使用。

情境對話1：

Ⓐ I'll never forgive that murderer.
我永遠都不會原諒那個兇手。

Ⓑ You're right! That beast ought to be sentenced to death!
沒有錯！那個禽獸應該被判死刑！

情境對話2：

Ⓐ If you betray us, I'll never forgive you.
如果你背叛了我們，我永遠不會原諒你。

Ⓑ Don't worry. I won't.
放心。我不會的。

字　彙

beast 野獸；畜生

betray 背叛

257. Just wait and see!

等著瞧!

說 明

當某人不相信你會成功或達成目標時，就可以用這句話告訴對方，表示假以時日，你可以做到的。

情境對話1：

Ⓐ Just wait and see! I'll come back one day when I succeed.

等著瞧！有一天當我成功時，我會回來的。

Ⓑ Good! I will wait for that day to come.

很好！我會等那一天到來的。

情境對話2：

Ⓐ It's impossible for you to acquire the Ph.D.

你不可能獲得博士學位的。

Ⓑ Just wait and see. Time will tell.

等著瞧。時間會證明一切的。

字 彙

acquire 獲取；得到

Ph.D. (Doctor of Philosophy)博士(學位)

258. Knock it off.

少來這一套。/別鬧了。

說 明

當你覺得某人做出讓你很討厭的事情時，例如，講話聲音太大或是吵架等，就可以用這句話告訴對方，請對方停止。

情境對話1：

Ⓐ They've been yelling, singing, and watching TV nonstop for days.
他們已經好幾天不停地喧囂、唱歌和看電視了。

Ⓑ Could someone tell them to knock it off?
有誰可以叫他們停止別鬧了嗎？

情境對話2：

Ⓐ Did you tell him to knock it off?
是你叫他別吵了嗎？

Ⓑ Yes, I did.
沒錯，是我。

字　彙

yell 叫喊　　　　　　　　　　nonstop 不停地

---

259. Leave me alone.　　　127

走開。

說　明

　　當你不希望被打擾時，或心情不好想一個人靜一靜時，就可以用這句話表示。但通常說這句話時，是帶著生氣的情緒。另外，此句另有他意，當說話者這麼說時，也可能代表"別理我"，或是"我不是好惹的，所以最好離我遠一點"的意思。

情境對話1：

Ⓐ Would you please leave me alone?
可以請你離開嗎？

Ⓑ Ok. I am leaving now.
好。我現在就離開。

情境對話2：

Ⓐ What do you say let's go to see a movie?
我們一起去看電影，你覺得如何呢？

Ⓑ Could you leave me alone? I am not in a good mood to see a movie now.
可以讓我一個人靜靜嗎？我現在沒心情看電影。

字　彙

mood 心情

---

260. Let go.

放手。

說　明

　當你不想要他人抓住你時，就可以用這句話告訴他。另外，當你看見對方因為某件事情難過、傷心或堅持某些事情而沉溺負面的情緒中時，也可以用這句話告訴對方，請他放下或忘掉不愉快的事情。

情境對話1：

Ⓐ Please let go of my hand, dad. I can cross the road by myself.
爸，請放開我的手。我可以自己過馬路。

Ⓑ Well, but I still worry about your safety.
可是我還是會擔心你的安全。

情境對話2：

Ⓐ I've regretted doing those things to Leo.
我一直好後悔對李歐所做的那些事情。

Ⓑ Just let go, James. You don't have any ability to change it, either.
詹姆斯，放手吧。你也沒有能力去改變。

字　彙

regret 後悔　　　　　　　　ability 能力

---

261. Look at this mess!　

看看這爛攤子！

說　明

當你看見或得知某事或某物的結果是個爛攤子時，就可以用這句話表示，讓他人知道你很生氣，而且有責備造成此結果的人之意。

情境對話 1：

Ⓐ Look at this mess! Who did it?
看看這爛攤子！是誰做的？

Ⓑ I don't know. I was not on the spot then.
我不知道。我當時不在現場。

情境對話 2：

Ⓐ Sir, I have bad news. The suspect we've been chasing disappeared.
長官，我有壞消息。我們一直追捕的嫌疑犯不見了。

Ⓑ Disappeared? Look at this mess! How should I tell this to Sheriff Dave?
不見了？看看這爛攤子！那我該怎麼把這件事告訴大衛警長呢？

字　彙

on the spot 現場　　　　　suspect 嫌疑犯

chase 追捕；追逐　　　　　disappear 消失、不見

sheriff 警長

262. Look what you've done!

看看你都做了些什麼！

說　明

當你知道是誰犯下的錯誤或搞砸事情、弄亂現場的環境時，就可以用這句話責罵對方，並請對方收拾善後，如果還有辦法善後的話。

情境對話1：

🅐 Look what you've done! Clean the living room now before the host comes back.
看看你做了些什麼！現在，在主人回來前把客廳清理乾淨！

🅑 Sorry. I'll do it right now.
對不起。我馬上去做。

情境對話2：

🅐 I made a huge mistake. I'm having an affair with my colleague.
我犯了一個嚴重的錯誤。我和我的同事發生外遇。

🅑 Gosh! Look what you've done!
天哪！看看你做了什麼！

字　彙

host 主人
huge 巨大的；非常的
affair 事件；風流韻事
colleague 同事

263. Mind your own business.

(129)

少管閒事。

說　明

　　當你發現對方有意無意的詢問、干涉或探問你個人的事情時，而讓你有不舒服的感覺時，甚至帶有生氣的情緒時，就可以用這句話告訴對方，表示你不希望被人探隱私。當然，只要對方是針對他人的事情做評斷或干涉時，你也可以用這句話告訴他，請他別插手別人的事情。

情境對話1：

Ⓐ This bag doesn't suit your age.
這個包包與你的年紀不相符。

Ⓑ Mind your own business. I just like it!
你管我。我就是喜歡它！

情境對話2：

Ⓐ Remember; mind your own business and you won't get into troubles.
記住，少管閒事，你就不會惹上麻煩。

Ⓑ Ok. I'll take a note of what you said.
好。我會把你所說的記下來。

字　彙

take a note of 把~記下來

264. My God!

我的天哪！

說　明

　　當你聽到或看到某件讓你驚訝的事情或畫面時，或是想起自己該處理而忘了處理的事情時，就可以用這句話。另外，遇到驚喜時，也可以用這句話表示。

情境對話1：

🅐 My God! Is this necklace my birthday gift?
我的天哪！這串項鍊是我的生日禮物嗎？

🅑 Yes. That is yours. Wear it now.
是的。那是你的了。現在就戴上它吧。

情境對話2：

🅐 Sharon, you passed the qualifying exam!
雪倫，你通過資格考了！

🅑 My God! I eventually did it! I feel so excited now!
我的天哪！我終於成功了！我現在覺得好興奮啊！

字　彙

qualifying　合格的

---

265. Shame on you! （130）

你真是丟臉！

說　明

當你發現你的朋友或家人、同事做了一件非常丟臉或可恥的事情時，就可以用這句話表示，但此句的語氣很重，是帶有責罵意味的。

情境對話1：

🅐 Why did you spread the rumor throughout the company? Shame on you!
為什麼你要把謠言傳遍整個公司？你真是丟臉！

情境對話2：

🅐 You shouldn't have done that! Shame on you!
你不應該這麼做的！你真是丟臉！

B I'm not the only one who did it. Frank also got involved in it.

我不是唯一做這件事的人。法蘭克也有。

字　彙	
spread　散播；傳遍	throughout　遍及；遍佈
shame　羞恥；恥辱	

266. Shut up!

閉嘴！

說　明

當你希望對方閉嘴時，就可以用這句話表示。但這句話適合用在熟識的人身上，因為此句話是不禮貌的用法。

情境對話1：

A Would you please shut up? You are so noisy that I can't hear the radio.

可以請你閉嘴嗎？你太吵了讓我無法聽到廣播。

B I'm sorry.

對不起。

情境對話2：

A Can you tell the kids to shut up? I can't concentrate on my work.

你可以叫那些小孩們閉嘴嗎？我無法專心工作。

B Hey, kids. Let's go out to fly a kite.

孩子們，我們到外面去放風箏吧。

字　彙	
radio　廣播電台；無線電	concentrate　專心
fly a kite　放風箏	

267. Stop complaining!

> 別發牢騷！

說　明

當你的朋友、家人或同事一直跟你抱怨事情，讓你感到厭煩時，就可以用這句話告訴他們，請他們別再發牢騷了。

情境對話1：

🅐 I need to tell you about my boss. She gives us lots of pressure and often asks us to work on the weekend. Besides, she also....
我必須告訴你關於我老闆。她給我們很多壓力，而且又常常要求我們週末去上班。此外，她還……。

🅑 Judy, stop complaining!
茱蒂，別再發牢騷了！

情境對話2：

🅐 The only way to success is to stop complaining about the predicaments or challenges you may encounter.
通向成功的唯一方式就是不要抱怨你所遇到的困境或是挑戰。

字　彙

predicament 困境；危境　　　encounter 遭遇；遇到

268. Stop fooling around!

> 別再混了！

說　明

若你的友人、同事或是家人等，常待在家裡無所事事，或是不專心於某事上時，又或是在工作、學業上等混水摸魚時，就可以用這句話告訴他們，請他們趕緊找工作或是專心於當前的事情上。

情境對話1：

Ⓐ Stop fooling around all day long at home!
別整天待在家裡混了！

Ⓑ I know. I've been trying hard to look for jobs.
我知道。我一直有努力去找工作了。

情境對話2：

Ⓐ It's work time so you'd better stop fooling around.
現在是上班時間，所以你最好別再混了。

Ⓑ Relax. He just left.
放輕鬆。他剛才離開。

字　彙

relax 放輕鬆

---

269. Take a hike!

哪兒涼快哪兒歇去吧！

說　明

當你和別人吵架時，尤其是熟識的人時，就可以用上這句話，類似中文"滾到一邊"的意思。

情境對話1：

Ⓐ Take a hike! I don't want to see you!
滾到一邊吧！我不想看見你！

Ⓑ I'm sorry. I know it's all my fault but I didn't mean it, please.
對不起。我知道都是我的錯，但我不是故意的，拜託。

情境對話2：

Ⓐ Don't you think that this gossip is truly funny and kind of ridiculous?

你不覺得這個八卦真的很好笑又有點荒謬嗎？

Ⓑ Take a hike. I'm not interested in those meaningless stuffs at all.

哪兒涼快哪兒歇去吧!我對這些沒營養的事一點興趣都沒有。

字　彙

hike　徒步旅行；遠足　　　　funny　可笑的；好笑的

ridiculous　荒謬的；滑稽的

---

270. **That's it！**

夠了！/就是這樣了！

說　明

　當對方所做的事情讓你看不下時，例如：所說的話激怒到你，或是開的玩笑太過火時，就可以用這句話。另外，當對方幫你盛食物的量，你覺得夠了時，也可以這麼說。

情境對話1：

Ⓐ Does this dress look great on me? And how about that one?

這件洋裝穿在我身上好看嗎？那麼那件呢？

Ⓑ That's it! Stop asking me.

夠了！別再問我了。

情境對話2：

Ⓐ A salad, a cup of black tea, and a cheese cake. Is there anything else?

一份沙拉，一杯紅茶，和一塊乳酪蛋糕。還有別的嗎？

B No, that's it.
不，這樣就好了。

字　彙

black tea 紅茶　　　　　else 其他；另外

---

271. That's terrible!

真糟糕！

說　明

當你覺得某件事的結果或情況看起來很糟糕時，就可以用這句話。

情境對話 1：

A Stan got rash all over his body after dinner.
史丹用完晚餐後就全身起疹子。

B That's terrible. Is he allergic to seafood?
真糟糕！他對海鮮過敏嗎？

情境對話 2：

A Did you see the earthquake and tsunami on TV in Japan?
你有看到電視播的日本地震和海嘯嗎？

B Yes, I saw it. That's terrible.
有，我有看到。真的很慘。

字　彙

rash 疹子；草率、魯莽的　　allergic 過敏的

seafood 海鮮　　　　　　　shrimp 蝦子

earthquake 地震　　　　　　tsunami 海嘯

272. What a pity!

真是可惜！

說　明

　若某件事的結果讓人有遺憾或可惜的感覺時，就可以用這句話表示。例如，差一分就可以得到獎品時，此句話就能派上用場。

情境對話1：

Ⓐ I failed the civil service exam by one point.
我差一分就能考上公務員考試。

Ⓑ What a pity!
真是太可惜了！

情境對話2：

Ⓐ Due to the car accident, Karen missed the opportunity to travel abroad.
由於車禍，凱倫錯過出國旅遊的機會。

Ⓑ What a pity!
真是可惜！

字　彙

point 分數；點
civil 市民的；公民的
service 服務
by 被；由；相差
travel 旅遊

273. What the heck!

(134)

管它的！

說　明

　這是非常口語的用法，類似的用法有 What the hell~?/ What on earth~?/ What in the world~?，中文可說成 "到底" 或 "究竟" 怎樣等等。但這種表示方式大多帶有生氣或是發牢騷的語氣。不建議用在正式場合中。

情境對話 1：

Ⓐ What the heck is the instruction? The words are so small and unclear.
這說明書到底是怎樣啊？字那麼小又不清楚。

Ⓑ Calm down. Let me see.
冷靜。讓我看看。

情境對話 2：

Ⓐ What the heck are you doing? Why did you tell them about my embarrassment?
你在搞什麼啊？你為什麼告訴他們我的糗事啊？

Ⓑ Of course not. I just made a slip of the tongue.
當然不是。我只是不小心說溜嘴。

字　彙

embarrassment 糗事；使人困窘的事

274. What a shame !

真可惜！

說　明

通常聽到一些壞消息或不幸的事情，我們會說 What a shame!表示感慨或嘆息。此句也可以用 What a pity!代替。

情境對話1：

Ⓐ Gary won a free cruise but he couldn't go.
蓋瑞贏得一張免費的郵輪船票，但他卻無法去。

Ⓑ What a shame!
那真是太可惜了！

情境對話2：

Ⓐ I could have been my best friend's bridesmaid, but I didn't.
我原本要當我最好朋友的伴娘，但卻沒當成。

Ⓑ What a shame!
真是可惜！

字　彙

cruise 郵輪
heavy 繁重的
bridesmaid 伴娘

275. Watch out!

(135)

當心！

說　明

　　Watch out!是警告別人要小心的意思。另外，在一些危急的情況下，就可用 Watch out!叫別人小心，所以此句的語氣帶有緊急之意，因此語氣也強過 Be careful.否則別人不會當心。所以，當你所處的環境或現場發生了某些帶有危險性質的事情時，就可以用這句話大喊說Watch out!以警示對方。例如，過馬路時，車子差點撞到對方時，就可以用這句話表示。還有一種情況，例如，你想警告你的女性朋友要小心她的男朋友時，也可以跟她說這句話，前提是因為你知道關於那男生的負面消息。

情境對話1：

Ⓐ Watch out for the car!
小心那輛車！

Ⓑ Thank you for calling me timely or I will get hit by the truck.
謝謝你及時叫住我，不然我就被卡車撞到。

情境對話2：

Ⓐ Watch out! You almost bumped the old lady!
小心！你差點撞到那位老太太！

Ⓑ Sorry! I didn't notice her.
對不起！我沒注意到她。

字　彙

timely　及時的；適時地

truck　卡車

276. You're a jerk!

你這個混蛋！

說　明

　這句話常用於罵人的時候，語氣非常的重，常用於熟人之間的吵架上。主詞可以換成任何人。

情境對話1：

Ⓐ You're a jerk! How could you throw my clothes from the balcony?
你這個混蛋！你怎麼可以把我的衣服從陽台上丟下去？

Ⓑ You did it to me first.
是你先這麼做的。

情境對話2：

Ⓐ Danny spread the rumor about me and even tried to blackmail me.
丹尼散佈關於我的謠言，而且甚至想勒索我。

Ⓑ He is a jerk! I suggest you should call the police.
他真是混蛋！我建議你應該去報警。

字　彙

balcony 陽臺　　　　　　　　spread 散播
blackmail 勒索；敲詐

277. You crack me up.

你把我笑死了。

說　明

　當對方所說的事或做的動作讓你覺得很好笑，或是讓你笑破肚皮時，就可以用上這句話。

情境對話1：

Ⓐ Let's go shopping! I need some new clothes.
一起去買東西吧！我需要一些新衣服。

Ⓑ You crack me up. You have three closets filled with the clothes.
你笑死我了，你已經有三個裝滿衣服的衣櫃。

情境對話2：

Ⓐ The joke you said really cracked me up. How could someone be so foolish?
你說的笑話真的是笑死我了。怎麼會有人這麼愚蠢呢？

Ⓑ Yeah, I can't believe it, either.
是啊，我也無法相信。

字　彙

crack【口語】說(笑話等)；爆裂；裂開

closet 衣櫃

foolish 愚蠢

278. You crossed the line.

你太過分了。

說　明

　　如果有人做了某些事或說了某些話，而觸怒了你心中所設定的標準時，就可以對他說 You crossed the line.(你太過份了)，或是說 You've gone too far. (你太離譜了)。

情境對話1：

Ⓐ You crossed the line when you said I eat like a pig.
你太過分了，說我吃得像一頭豬。

Ⓑ But you had just finished a loaf of toast in ten minutes.
但你剛才真的在十分鐘內吃完一整條土司。

情境對話2：

Ⓐ You crossed the line! How could you read my letter without my permission?
你太過分了！你怎麼可以沒經過我的允許就看我的信呢？

Ⓑ I thought it was an advertisement letter.
我以為它是廣告信。

字　彙

loaf 一條或一塊(麵包)　　　toast 土司

---

279. **You deserve it!**

活該！/你應得的！

說　明

此句可用於正面或負面的用法。正面，例如：你的某位同事或朋友辛苦工作多年，終於獲得老闆賞識而升遷或加薪，就可以用此句表示 "你應得的"。反之，某人作奸犯科，最後落入法網，也可以此句表示 "活該"。

情境對話1：

Ⓐ Finally, after two years working in the company I got a promotion and a raise on the salary.
終於，在這間公司工作兩年之後，我獲得升遷及加薪。

Ⓑ You deserve it. After all, you spend all your time on your job.
這是你應得的。畢竟，你幾乎都把你的時間花在工作上。

情境對話2：

Ⓐ The cruel murderer was caught by the police last night.
那個殘忍的兇手昨天晚上被警方逮住。

Ⓑ He deserves it. He should be put into jail.
他活該。他應該被抓去坐牢。

字　彙

jail 監獄

280. You have a lot of nerve.

你臉皮真厚。

說　明

當你發現你的友人很厚臉皮時，就可以用這上這句話。

情境對話1：

Ⓐ You have a lot of nerve. How dare you talk to the manager in such an impolite way?
你臉皮真厚。你怎麼膽敢用這麼不禮貌的方式跟經理講話？

Ⓑ I just spoke out my mind.
我只是說出心裡話而已。

情境對話2：

Ⓐ I bargained with the salesman in the store of fixed price yesterday.
我昨天在不二價店裡和業務員殺價。

Ⓑ Wow, you have a lot of nerve.
哇，你臉皮真厚。

字　彙

nerve 神經　　　　　　　impolite 不禮貌的

bargain 討價還價　　　　fixed price 不二價；固定價

281. You make me sick!

你真讓我感到噁心！

說　明

當對方所做的事情或所説的話讓你感到很噁心、不舒服時，就可以用這句話表示，請他別再説或別再做了。

情境對話1：

ⓐ You make me sick! Why did you put the used tissue into the drawer?

你真讓我感到噁心！你為什麼要把用過的衛生紙放進抽屜裡？

ⓑ Don't worry. I'll clean it later, ok?

別擔心。我待會清理，好嗎？

情境對話2：

ⓐ You used these innocent children to trade drugs. You really make me sick!

你利用這些無辜的小孩來交易毒品。你真讓我感到噁心！

ⓑ So are you going to sue me?

所以你要告我嗎？

字　彙

drawer 抽屜

innocent 無辜的

trade 交易；貿易

sue 控告

282. You piss me off.

你氣死我了。

說　明

當對方所做的事情或所説的話讓你很生氣時，就可以用這句話。

情境對話1：

Ⓐ You piss me off! Get out of here!
你氣死我了！給我滾開！

Ⓑ Why? I didn't mean to do it. It's just a coincidence.
為什麼？我又不是故意的。那純屬巧合。

Ⓐ No more excuses for your repeated mistakes on the same thing!
不要再為你重蹈覆轍的錯誤找藉口！

情境對話2：

Ⓐ What would happen if I keep teasing you?
如果我一直戲弄你會怎樣？

Ⓑ Well, you'll piss me off.
那麼你就會讓我生氣。

字　彙

coincidence 巧合　　　　　repeated 重覆的
tease 戲弄；挑逗

283. You set me up!

139

你出賣我！

說　明

當你發現你相信的人在背後捅你一刀或出賣、背叛你時，就可以用這句話表示，那麼你通常就會和對方決裂，不再互相往來。

情境對話1：

Ⓐ You set me up! How could you do this to me?
你出賣我！你怎能這樣對我呢？

Ⓑ You set me up two years ago as well. Don't you remember?
你兩年前也出賣我。你不記得了嗎？

情境對話2：

Ⓐ I've treated you like my own family, but it turned out that you set me up. Why?
我待你如我的家人一般，結果你卻出賣我。為什麼？

Ⓑ I'm sorry but I have no choice.
對不起，但我別無選擇。

字 彙

turn out 結果是

284. You're headed for trouble.

你會惹上麻煩。

說 明

當你眼見你的友人可能會因為他不好的習慣或個性、言行舉止等，而惹上麻煩時，就可以用這句話提醒或警告他。而本句裡的 head 是指 "向~的方向"。

情境對話1：

Ⓐ You're headed for trouble if you don't get rid of your bad habit.
如果你不改掉你的壞習慣，你會惹上麻煩。

B Which bad habit do you mean?
你是指什麼壞習慣？

情境對話2：

A You're headed for trouble if you don't leave now.
如果你現在不走，你會惹上麻煩的。

B No. I have the responsibility for this matter. I can't leave.
不。這件事我有責任。我不能走。

字 彙

get rid of 戒除

habit 習慣

Chapter 4

表達支持、讚美或安慰用語

285. Cheer up!

> 振作點！

說　明

　　當你看見你的友人因為挫折而垂頭喪氣時，就可以用這句話告訴他，請他鼓起精神，振作點。

情境對話1：

Ⓐ What's wrong? You look so frustrated.
怎麼了？你看起來很沮喪。

Ⓑ Kate just left me but I still love her deeply.
凱特離我而去了，但我還是深愛著她。

Ⓐ Cheer up! Life goes on.
振作點！生活還是得繼續下去呀。

情境對話2：

Ⓐ Cheer up! It's just a small failure. We can carry on again.
振作點！這只是小小的失敗而已。我們可以再繼續。

Ⓑ You're right. We can start it over again.
你說得對。我們可以重新再來一次。

字　彙

failure 失敗　　　　　　　　carry on 繼續

286. Congratulations!

> 恭喜！

說　明

　　當你聽到別人的好消息或喜訊時，就可以用這句話表示，例如：結婚、升遷、搬新家、金榜題名……等等。

情境對話1：

Ⓐ I heard that your daughter will get married this June. Congratulations!
我聽說你的女兒今年六月就要結婚了。恭喜呀！

Ⓑ Thank you! I'll send you a wedding invitation and hope you can come to the wedding as well.
謝謝你！我會寄喜帖給你，也希望你能來參加婚禮。

情境對話2：

Ⓐ Congratulations on your new house!
祝你新居落成！

Ⓑ Thanks for your compliments.
謝謝你的祝賀！

字　彙

wedding invitation　喜帖　　　　compliments　致意；道賀

287. Don't give up!

別放棄！

說　明

當你的友人看似要放棄他所在乎的事物時，就可以用這句話鼓勵他，希望他能再努力點，或再堅持一下，就可以成功了，不要輕易放棄。

情境對話1：

Ⓐ I can't continue this without Dianne. It's so hard!
沒有黛安，我無法繼續下去。太難了！

Ⓑ Don't give up! If she were here, she wouldn't want to see you this way.
別放棄！如果她還在的話，她不會想看到這樣的你。

情境對話2：

Ⓐ Don't give up easily! We've gone so far.
別輕易放棄！我們已經走了這麼遠。

Ⓑ But I have no strength now. I need to take a rest for a while.
但我現在沒有力氣。我需要休息一會兒。

字　彙

strength　力氣

288. Don't sweat it!

別緊張！

說　明

sweat 本身指 "出汗" 或 "汗水" 的意思，通常緊張時，人多少會冒汗，所以這句話引申為別緊張。當你的友人要上台報告或表演時，他看起來很緊張時，就可以跟他說這句話，也可以說 Take a deep breath.(深吸一口氣)或是 Relax.(放輕鬆。)

情境對話1：

Ⓐ Tomorrow I'm going to deliver a speech in a university. I feel quite nervous.
明天我就要在一所大學發表演講。我好緊張。

Ⓑ Don't sweat it. You'll get used to it.
別緊張。你會習慣的。

情境對話2：

Ⓐ Don't sweat it! Try to pretend as naturally as you can.
別緊張！盡你所能裝得愈自然愈好。

Ⓑ Ok, I got it!
好，我瞭解。

字　彙

deliver 發表　　　　　　　pretend 假裝
naturally 自然地

289. Don't take it so hard.

別看得太嚴重。

說　明

當你的友人或同事等，因為某些事情而想不開、給自己很大的壓力或自尋煩惱時，就可以用這句話鼓勵安慰他們，希望他們能適度減壓，不要把事情看得太嚴重，而應輕鬆一點，樂觀一點。

情境對話1：

Ⓐ I just failed my driving test and I really want to drive to work every day.

我剛剛考駕照失敗，我真的想每天開車上班。

Ⓑ Don't take it so hard. You can always take the test again.

別看得太嚴重，你可以重考。

情境對話2：

Ⓐ I didn't pass the oral test for entering the art college.

我沒有通過進入藝術學院的口試。

Ⓑ Don't take it so hard. You still have other options.

別想得太嚴重，你還有其他的選擇。

字　彙

driving 開車的
college 大學院校
option 選擇

290. Don't worry.

別擔心。

說　明

當你看見你的朋友、同事或家人等擔心其工作或某些事情時，就可以用這句話安慰他們，因為擔心也沒用！

情境對話1：

Ⓐ I haven't found my son for three days.
三天了，我還是找不到我的兒子。

Ⓑ Don't worry. We've sent more policemen to search your son.
別擔心。我們已經派更多警力來搜尋您的兒子。

情境對話2：

Ⓐ Don't worry. I have jotted down the number of the car and already called the police.
別擔心。我已經記下那台車的號碼，也已經打電話給警察了。

Ⓑ Thanks for your help.
謝謝你的幫忙。

字　彙

jot down 快速記下

291. Don't yell at me!

別對我大吼大叫！

說　明

當對方和你在講話時，忽然對你大吼時，可能他不是針對你，但你就可以用這句話告訴他，請他不要把颱風尾掃到你，或把氣出在你身上。當然，吵架的時候這句話更可以派上用場。

情境對話1：

Ⓐ Hey, man. Don't yell at me.
嘿，不要對我大吼大叫。

Ⓑ I'm sorry. I'm just too irritated when I think of that nuisance.
對不起。當我想到那個討厭鬼時，我就會太激動。

情境對話2：

Ⓐ Why didn't you inform me beforehand?
你為什麼不事先通知我？

Ⓑ Don't yell at me! I did but you didn't hear me then.
別對我大吼大叫！我有通知你，但你當時沒有聽到。

字　彙

nuisance　討厭的人或事物；麻煩事
inform　通知

292. Enjoy yourself!

祝你玩得開心！

說　明

當你的友人要去旅遊、參加派對，或是從事具娛樂性質活動的時候，就可以用上這句話，以示祝對方玩得愉快，類似 Have fun!

情境對話1：

Ⓐ I can't believe that Jennis invited me to the prom. I need to be dressed-up.
我不敢相信珍妮絲邀請我參加舞會。我得好好打扮一番了。

Ⓑ Congratulations. Enjoy yourself!
恭喜。祝你玩得開心啊！

情境對話2：

A Enjoy yourself and don't forget my present!
祝你玩得開心，還有別忘了我的禮物啊！

B I won't forget. See you!
我不會忘記的。再見！

字 彙

prom(常用於美國高中的)舞會　dressed-up 精心打扮的

293. Give it a try!

試看看吧！

說 明

當你遇到某個你不擅長的領域時，例如：打網球、做蛋糕或是烹飪……等，但你願意嘗試時，就可以說 Ok, I would give it a try.(好吧，我來試看看好了。) 當然，此句話也可以用來鼓勵別人。

情境對話1：

A Can you play tennis?
你會打網球嗎？

B No, I can't. I'm not good at tennis, but I would give it a try.
不，我不會打。我不擅長網球，但我願意試看看。

情境對話2：

A Just give it a try, Alex! You have the potential to overcome any difficulty.
艾利克斯，你就試看看吧！你有克服任何困難的潛力。

B Well, I think you overestimate me.
我想你高估我了。

字 彙

tennis 網球
potential 潛在的；潛力
overcome 克服
overestimate 對~評價(估計)過高

294. God bless you!

願上帝保佑你！

說 明

　　當你的朋友、家人或同事要從事某件你覺得需要有勇氣去做的事情，或是困難的挑戰時，就可以用這句話祝福他，希望他真能完成任務或挑戰。

情境對話1：

Ⓐ Goodbye and may God bless you.

　　再見，願上帝保佑你。

Ⓑ Thank you. I do hope so.

　　謝謝。我也希望如此。

情境對話2：

Ⓐ I have no choice but to enroll in military service for three years first.

　　我沒有辦法只好先服三年的兵役。

Ⓑ God bless you! Don't lose contact.

　　願上帝保佑你！別失去聯絡。

字 彙

enroll 登記；入伍；徵召
military service 兵役
contact 連絡；聯繫；接觸

295. Good luck!

祝你好運！

說　明

　當你的朋友或家人要去參加考試、求職或求婚時，就可以用這句話告訴他們，祝他們好運。

情境對話1：

Ⓐ Tomorrow, I am going to take the entrance exam.
明天我就要考入學考試了。

Ⓑ Good luck! Relax and do it as usual. I think you'll be doing great.
祝你好運。放輕鬆，就如同往常一樣。我想你會有不錯的表現。

情境對話2：

Ⓐ I plan to propose to Ann at the movie theater so don't tell her. Ok?
我打算在電影院跟安求婚，所以不要告訴她。好嗎？

Ⓑ Ok. I won't. Good luck!
好的。我不會說的。祝你好運啊！

字　彙

propose　求婚

296. Grow up!

成熟點吧！

說　明

　當你在跟你的朋友、家人或同事相處一段時間後，忽然發覺對方的個性、態度或想法等，沒那麼理性或成熟時，甚至帶有過於夢幻或是幼稚的感覺時，就可以用這句話表示。

情境對話1：

Ⓐ Grow up, Kevin! Don't think about things that are unrealistic.

成熟點吧，凱文！不要想那些不切實際的事了。

Ⓑ But with dreams, people can have the motive to realize their ideals.

但是有了夢想，人們才有動力實現他們的理想。

情境對話2：

Ⓐ I don't want to join Ellis's team.

我不想加入艾利斯那一組。

Ⓑ Grow up! You should put the work as a top priority.

成熟點吧！你應該把工作視為優先考量的事。

字　彙

unrealistic 不切實際的　　　　realize 實現
ideals 理想

297. Have a good time!

玩得愉快啊！

說　明

　　當你的友人要出去玩或是旅遊時，就可以用上這句話，表示玩得愉快。此句等於 Have fun!(玩得開心！)若要表示和某人玩得愉快，就在此句後面加上 with (表示和)。

情境對話1：

Ⓐ See you, grandfather! I'll come back soon.

再見了，爺爺！我很快就會回來。

Ⓑ Take care of yourself and have a good time!

你自己要多保重，且要玩得愉快啊！

情境對話2：

Ⓐ How was your trip to visit your pal in Switzerland?
你這趟去瑞士拜訪朋友之旅如何呢？

Ⓑ I had a good time with Laura's family. They are all friendly and hospitable.
我和蘿拉的家人玩得很愉快。他們都很友善而且好客。

字　彙

pal(口語)夥伴；好友　　　Switzerland 瑞士

hospitable 好客的

298. I'm on your side.

我支持你。

說　明

　當你想對你家人、朋友或同事所說的事情或意見表示支持的態度時，就可以用這句話。

情境對話1：

Ⓐ I seldom go out with my friends, but my wife always says that I spend too much time on them.
我很少和我的朋友出去，但我老婆卻總是說我花太多時間在朋友身上。

Ⓑ I'm on your side because you hardly call me to have a drink.
我支持你，因為你很少找我去喝一杯。

情境對話2：

Ⓐ I'm definitely on your side no matter what you say.
不論你說什麼我絕對支持你。

B Really? Even though when I go bankrupt?

真的嗎？即使當我破產時？

字　彙

seldom 幾乎不；極少　　　　have a drink 喝酒
go bankrupt 破產

299. I'm proud of you!

我以你為榮！

說　明

當你的朋友、家人或同事等，做了一件讓你覺得很了不起或很光榮的事情時，就可以跟他說這句話，表示你很以他為榮。

情境對話1：

A Dad, I am the champion of the national composition contest.

爸，我贏得全國作文比賽的優勝。

B You're so excellent! I'm proud of you!

你真是太優秀了！我以你為榮！

情境對話2：

A I'm really proud of you because you did something that no one could compete with you.

我真的以你為榮，因為你做了無人能與你媲美的事。

B Really? What did I do?

真的嗎？我做了什麼？

字　彙

national 全國的；國家的　　　composition 作文
excellent 優異的　　　　　　 compete 競爭

300. I agree.

我同意。

說　明

　如果你想對別人表示贊同和好感，就可以等他發表完意見後跟他說這句話。此句的原文是 I agree with you.

情境對話1：

Ⓐ Don't you think it would be more convenient to have your own car?
你不覺得你有一輛自己的車子會方便許多嗎？

Ⓑ I agree.
我同意。

情境對話2：

Ⓐ What do you say if we cooperate to defeat our same rival?
如果我們一起合作擊敗我們共同的敵人，你覺得如何呢？

Ⓑ I agree. Let's do it!
我贊成。我們就這麼做吧！

字　彙

convenient 方便的　　　　　defeat 擊敗
rival 對手；敵人

301. I can't agree with you more.

我非常同意你說的。

說　明

　當某人的意見或看法讓你非常認同時，或你的看法與之一致時，就可以用這句話告訴對方，以示贊同。

情境對話1：

Ⓐ I consider that we should go home earlier today.

我認為我們今天應該早點回家。

Ⓑ I can't agree with you more.

我非常同意你説的。

情境對話2：

Ⓐ I can't agree with you more. So, let's get started!

我非常同意你説的。那麼，我們就開始動工吧！

Ⓑ Really? Thanks for supporting me, sir.

真的嗎？謝謝你的支持，長官。

字　彙

consider 考慮；認為

---

302. I just want to help you.

我只想幫你而已。

說　明

當你想幫助你的朋友、家人或同事時，卻被拒絕好意，或對方不領情時，就可以用這句話表示你只是出自於一片好心想幫忙而已。

情境對話1：

Ⓐ Thank you. I accept your kindness but I can do it on my own.

謝謝你。你的好意我心領了，但我自己做得來。

Ⓑ Ok. I just want to help you.

好吧。我只是想幫你而已。

情境對話2：

Ⓐ No offense, but it's not your business.
我沒有惡意，但請不要插手我的事。

Ⓑ Fine. I just want to help you.
算了。我只是想幫忙而已。

字　彙

offense 冒犯；罪過

---

303. I know you can do it.

我相信你可以的。

說　明

這句話可以用來鼓勵對方，尤其當對方覺得自己沒有信心克服困難，或完成任務時。

情境對話1：

Ⓐ I'm not confident in that contest. There are five days only to the deadline.
我對那競賽沒有信心。距離截止日期只有五天。

Ⓑ I know you can do it. I have faith in you.
我相信你可以的。我對你有信心。

情境對話2：

Ⓐ I know you can do it as long as you try your best!
我相信你可以的，只要你盡力去做！

Ⓑ I'm glad to hear that.
我很高興聽到你這麼説。

字　彙

confident 有信心的　　　　　　deadline 期限；截止日期

304. Indeed.

的確。

說　明

　此句等於 That's right! (沒錯！)、Certainly!(確實如此！)用來表示證實或贊同、承認對方所說的事情。

情境對話1：

Ⓐ Did he leave without saying a word?
　他一句話都沒說就走了嗎？

Ⓑ Yes, indeed.
　是的，的確如此。

情境對話2：

Ⓐ I'm so starving, indeed.
　我真的快餓死了。

Ⓑ Ok, let's get something to eat. How about instant noodles?
　好吧，那我們來找點吃的東西吧。泡麵如何呢？

字　彙

starving 飢餓的　　　　　　　instant noodles 泡麵(速食麵)

305. It's worth a try.

值得一試。

說　明

　當某件事情是值得嘗試時，就可以用這句話跟對方表示，因為機不可失。

情境對話1：

A It's worth a try to launch a new business. Don't you think so?

創業是一件值得一試的事。你不覺得嗎？

B But it's risky. We don't have enough capital.

但風險太大了。我們沒有足夠的資金。

情境對話2：

A What do you say if we sell ice cream in summer and hot pot in winter ?

你覺得我們夏天賣冰淇淋，冬天賣火鍋如何呢？

B That sounds good. It's worth a try.

聽起來不錯。值得一試。

字　彙

launch 開辦；發起　　　　capital 資金

hot pot 火鍋

---

306. Just do it!

做就是了。

說　明

此句話可以用來鼓勵或給對方加油打氣，讓對方知道，做就是了，不要想太多或因為其他瑣事等而裹足不前。

情境對話1：

A Just do it! Vincent! Don't hesitate.

做就是了！文森！不要猶豫。

B Ok. I see.

好。我明白了。

情境對話2：

Ⓐ I'm not sure if I could pass the oral test.
我不確定我是否能通過口試。

Ⓑ Just do it! You've prepared so long, right?
做就是了！你已經準備這麼久了，不是嗎？

字　彙

oral test　口試

307. Keep it up!

堅持下去！

說　明

當你的友人在從事某件任務或事情時，眼看他快達成時，可是他看起來很痛苦或是有放棄的樣子時，就可以用這句話給他加油打氣，表示再撐一下就可以成功了。

情境對話1：

Ⓐ God! It's so hot and we still have a long way to go.
天哪！天氣這麼熱而我們還有一大段路要走。

Ⓑ Keep it up! We are almost there.
堅持下去！我們快到了。

情境對話2：

Ⓐ Keep it up, Raymond! One more loop, you can get the terminal line.
堅持下去呀，雷蒙！再一圈，你就可以到終點線了。

字　彙

loop　圈　　　　　　　　　terminal　終點的

308. Keep the change.

不用找了。

說　明

當你買東西時，想跟店員說不用找剩下的錢時，就可以用這句話表示。

情境對話1：

Ⓐ The total is 528 dollars, sir.
先生，總共是528元。

Ⓑ Here it is. Keep the change.
錢在這。不用找錢了。

情境對話2：

Ⓐ Keep the change.
不用找了。

Ⓑ Thank you, madam.
謝謝你，夫人。

字　彙

change 零錢

309. Keep your pants on.

沉住氣，忍耐點。

說　明

當你的友人被某件事情或其他人給激怒時，此時就可以趕快告訴他這句話，叫他忍著點、沉住氣，別發脾氣或是壞了大局。

情境對話1：

Ⓐ Wesley, keep your pants on. Don't lose your temper.
衛斯理，沉住氣。別發脾氣。

Ⓑ But look what he did to my best friend! I will never forgive him!
但你看他對我最好的朋友做了什麼！我絕不會原諒他！

情境對話2：

Ⓐ His letter irritated me a lot. I need to see him right now!
他的信真的是惹惱了我。我現在就要去見他！

Ⓑ Keep your pants on. Maybe it's a trap.
沉住氣。也許這是個陷阱。

字　彙

temper 脾氣　　　　　　　　irritate 使惱怒；使煩躁

---

310. Let it be!

就讓它去吧！

說　明

　　有些事情是天生注定無法改變時，或是無法挽回的結果時，就只能看開點，隨它去。因此，若你的友人遇到類似這樣的問題時，就可以用這句話告訴他。

情境對話1：

Ⓐ I made a call to the gas company to complain about our hot water.
我打電話給天然氣公司，跟他們投訴說我們沒有熱水。

Ⓑ Let it be! I did that last week.
隨它去吧！我上星期也這麼做。

情境對話2：

Ⓐ Let it be! You deserve better.
隨它去吧！你值得更好的。

Ⓑ I know, but it's not easy to forget my ex-boyfriend.
我知道，但是要忘記我前男友不是一件容易的事情。

字　彙
gas 瓦斯

---

311. Not bad.

還不賴。

說　明

這句話非常口語，當你覺得對方所做的事情或是提出的觀念、意見等，還蠻不錯時，就可以用這句話表示。在某種程度上，是一種表示認同，但也有些人覺得自己做得這麼好，卻只得到 Not bad.的稱讚，似乎還算不上是種肯定或讚美。

情境對話1：

Ⓐ What do you think about the concept I mentioned at the meeting?
你覺得我在會議上所提出的概念如何呢？

Ⓑ Not bad. It seems practicable.
還不錯。看起來似乎是可行的。

情境對話2：

Ⓐ I saw the musical at your school last Saturday. It's not bad.
我上星期六看了你學校的音樂劇。還挺不錯的。

Ⓑ Really?
真的嗎？

字　彙

practicable 可實行的　　　　　musical 音樂的；歌舞劇

---

312. Seize the time.

把握時間。

說　明

當你想跟對方表示時間有限，所以要趕緊在時限內完成任務或是及時行樂時，都可以用上這句話。

情境對話1：

Ⓐ Everyone should seize the time .
每個人都應該把握時間。

Ⓑ That's right. Because life is short.
沒錯。因為人生短暫。

情境對話2：

Ⓐ After I finish the report, I 'll see my favorite serial.
當我完成報告後，我要看我最愛的連續劇。

Ⓑ It will rebroadcast every Thursday night. You should seize the time doing something valuable.
你應該把握時間做些有價值的事情。

字　彙

seize 抓住
serial 連續的；連續劇
valuable 有價值的

每日一句 生活英語
Everyday English

313. Take it easy.

155

放輕鬆。

說　明

　如果你有認識的朋友是屬於急性子的人，或是個性非常激動、容易緊張的話，就可以告訴他這句話，請他放鬆。

情境對話 1：

Ⓐ I was preparing the statistics presentation last night and didn't sleep well.
我昨晚準備統計學的報告，所以沒有睡好。

Ⓑ Take it easy. If you don't get enough sleep, you won't perform well.
放輕鬆。如果你沒有足夠的睡眠，就不會有好的表現。

情境對話 2：

Ⓐ Take it easy. Don't you know "Haste makes waste?"
放輕鬆。你不知道 "欲速則不達嗎？"

字　彙

statistics 統計(學)　　　　　presentation 呈現；報告

perform 表現

314. Take your time.

別急，慢慢來。

說　明

　當你的朋友或同事因為突如其來的事情或工作，而必須趕在時間期限之前完成，但已經來不及完成時，就可以用這句話告訴他。或者是，某件工作所需完成的時間還很長，但你的朋友或同事卻整天憂慮，不知該從何著手時，也可以用這句話告訴他，表示時間多的是，慢慢來，說不定就能想到辦法解決。

情境對話1：

Ⓐ I've got to go now. My flight leaves at 8:30 this morning.
我現在必須走了。我的飛機今早八點半就要起飛了。

Ⓑ Just take your time. You can take a taxi and get to the airport in 30 minutes.
別急，慢慢來。你搭計程車三十分鐘內就可以到機場。

情境對話2：

Ⓐ What should I do now? I left my suitcase in the airplane.
我現在該怎麼辦？我把公事包留在飛機上。

Ⓑ Calm down and take your time.
冷靜下來，不要急。

字　彙

suitcase　公事包；手提箱

---

315. Thank you for your advice.

謝謝你的建議。

說　明

　　當對方提出的建議讓你有所獲益或啟發時，就可以用這句話以表示你對他的感謝。

情境對話1：

Ⓐ Thank you for your advice. It helped a lot to my work.
謝謝你的建議。它真的對我的工作幫助很多。

Ⓑ Really? I'm glad I can help you.
真的嗎？我很高興我能幫上你的忙。

情境對話2：

Ⓐ How was your presentation last Wednesday?
你上週三的報告如何呢？

Ⓑ Good. Thank you for your advice.
很好。謝謝你的建議。

字　彙

advice　勸告；建議

---

316. That's a good idea. 〔156〕

那真是個好主意。

說　明

　當對方所提出的意見或想法，你覺得不錯，是個可實行的方法時，就可以用上這句話，表示贊同。

情境對話1：

Ⓐ Let's go rent a car to travel around southern Taiwan this summer!
今年夏天我們來租車子環遊南台灣吧！

Ⓑ That's a good idea.
那真是個好主意。

情境對話2：

Ⓐ Since it's raining heavily today, how about watching some movies at home?
既然今天雨下那麼大，不如在家看電影，你覺得呢？

Ⓑ I agree. That's a good idea.
我贊成。那真是個好主意。

字　彙

rent 租   southern 南部的；南邊的

since 既然   heavily 嚴重地；猛烈地

---

317. That's so kind of you.

你真好。

說　明

　　當對方幫了你一個大忙時，或是很體貼地幫你做了一些事情，但當時你可能不知道，或是事後才知道對方幫你處理了一些事情，此時就可以用這句話告訴他，以表示你對他的感謝。

情境對話1：

Ⓐ I've already cleaned the conference room and prepared all the files you need.
我已經清理過會議室，也把你要的資料準備好了。

Ⓑ That's so kind of you.
你真好。

情境對話2：

Ⓐ Who bought this gorgeous cake? It looks so great and delicious.
是誰買了這個這麼豪華的蛋糕？它看起來很棒且很好吃的樣子。

Ⓑ It's me.
是我買的。

Ⓐ That's so kind of you.
你真好。

字　彙

gorgeous 華麗的；豪華的

318. **That sounds great!**

那聽起來不錯啊！

說 明

　當你覺得你的友人所敘述的事情讓你覺得很棒或很羨慕時，就可以用此句表達。

情境對話1：

Ⓐ We're going to go on a honeymoon to Bali Island.
我們將要去峇里島度蜜月。

Ⓑ That sounds great. When will you go?
聽起來很棒。你們什麼時候要去？

情境對話2：

Ⓐ That sounds great for you to move to the suburbs. But I will miss you very much.
你要搬去郊區聽起來很不錯。但我會很想念你的。

Ⓑ Me, too. Let's keep in touch, ok?
我也是。我們要保持聯絡，好嗎？

字 彙

honeymoon (度)蜜月　　　　Bali Island 峇里島

suburb 郊區

319. **Well done!**

做得好！/全熟。

說 明

　當你的朋友把事情做得好，或做了善事就可以用這句話稱讚他，就等於Good job.。另外，當你去吃牛排時，服務生問你的牛排要幾分熟時，若你想吃全熟時，就可以用這句話回答他。

情境對話1：

Ⓐ Yesterday morning on the bus, I yielded a seat to an elderly woman.

昨天早上在公車上時，我讓位給一個老太太。

Ⓑ Well done! You are so kind.

做得好！你人真好。

情境對話2：

Ⓐ Sir, how would you like your steak? Rare? Medium? Medium well or well done?

先生，你希望你的牛排幾分熟？三分熟？五分熟？七分熟還是全熟？

Ⓑ Well done, please.

全熟，謝謝。

字　彙

yield 讓；屈服；產出	elderly 年長的
steak 牛排	rare 稀有罕見的；三分熟
medium 五分熟	medium well 七分熟

320. You're looking sharp! 158

你看上去真棒。

說　明

當你的友人穿了一件新衣服或有新的裝扮時，而的確他的穿著也很不賴時，就可以用這句話以示讚美。

情境對話1：

Ⓐ You're looking sharp in that new outfit!

你穿那套衣服看上去真棒！

B Thank you! I like it, too.
謝謝你！我也很喜歡這衣服。

情境對話2：

A Look! What do you think about my new jacket and sunglasses?
你看！你覺得我的新夾克和太陽眼鏡如何？

B Well, you're looking sharp! You must have spent a lot of money on them.
你看上去真棒！你一定花了很多錢買吧。

字　彙

outfit 全套服裝(工具或裝備)	sharp 時髦的；漂亮的
jacket 夾克外套	sunglasses 太陽眼鏡

321. You bet!

你說得對！

說　明

此句等於 You're right! Bingo! 亦即你說對了，或是你說中了的意思。

情境對話1：

A Are you afraid of cockroaches and spiders?
你怕蟑螂和蜘蛛嗎？

B You bet! They make me feel gross.
你說對了！他們讓我感到噁心。

情境對話2：

A You bet! I'm not really into Paul.
你說得對！我其實沒那麼愛保羅。

B But you're going to get married next month!
但你們下個月就要結婚了！

字　彙

spider 蜘蛛　　　　　　　　　gross(口語)令人噁心的、討厭的
into 對~熱中、入迷

---

322. You did a good job.　　(159)

你做得非常好。

說　明

當你知道有人表現很好或有不錯的成績時，就可以用這句話表示鼓勵及讚美。

情境對話1：

A You did a good job so we would like to reward you. What would you like?
你做得非常好，所以我們想要犒賞你。你想要什麼？

B Actually, I just want fifteen days off to go on a vacation.
其實，我只想有15天的假期來渡假。

情境對話2：

A I finally defeated my opponent and got the championship!
我終於打敗我的對手並取得冠軍！

B Wow, you did a good job! It's really not easy!
哇，你做得太棒了！這真的很不簡單啊！

字　彙

reward 報償；獎賞　　　　　　vacation 假期
opponent 對手；敵人

323. You did right.

你做得對。

說 明

當你的友人所做的事情是正確、合理的，儘管被其他人反對，此時就可以用這句話告訴他，表示他所做的事情是合乎情理或是正確的。

情境對話1：

Ⓐ I told Lexie to hand in her assignment on time, but she scolded me.
我告訴萊西要準時交作業，但她卻罵我。

Ⓑ You did right! It's her problem.
你做得對！那是她的問題。

情境對話2：

Ⓐ You did right. We should tear down that illegal building.
你做得對。我們應該拆除這棟違建物。

Ⓑ So, what's the next step?
那麼，下一步是什麼？

字 彙

tear down 拆除

324. You have my word. 🎧160

我會遵守承諾。

說 明

當你答應或承諾對方時，為了以示你會做到時，就可以用這句話告訴對方。

情境對話1：

Ⓐ Are you sure you can fulfil your responsibility to this company?
你確定你可以盡到對這公司的責任嗎？

Ⓑ You have my word.
我會遵守承諾的。

情境對話2：

Ⓐ You have my word. I'll keep them in my mind.
我會遵守承諾的。我會把他們牢記心裡的。

Ⓑ I hope you do so as well.
我也希望你能做到。

字　彙

fulfil 履行；實現

325. You impress me!

你讓我印象深刻！

說　明

當某人所做的事情或演說、表演等，讓你印象深刻時，就可以告訴對方這句話。這句話可用在正面或負面的評價上。

情境對話1：

Ⓐ You impress me, Jane! I never thought that you could dance so well and beautifully.
珍，你讓我印象深刻！我從未想到你可以跳得這麼棒又這麼漂亮。

Ⓑ Thank you. I really appreciate your praise.
謝謝你。我真的很感謝你的稱讚。

情境對話2：

Ⓐ The student impressed me most unfavorably for his indecent attitude.
那位學生不禮貌的態度給我極差的印象。

Ⓑ Do you mean that boy in white?
你是指那個穿白色衣服的男生嗎？

字　彙

praise 稱讚　　　　　　　　　unfavorably 令人不悅的

indecent 不禮貌的；粗魯的

326. You really helped me out!

你真的幫了我！

說　明

　某人在你正需要幫助時忽然給你一臂之力，或是幫了你，是你沒有預料之內時，就可以用這句話告訴對方以示感激。

情境對話1：

Ⓐ Peter, I sent your car to the auto factory to be repaired.
彼得，我把你的車送到修車廠維修去了。

Ⓑ You really helped me out! Thanks a lot.
你真的幫了我！多謝啦！

情境對話2：

Ⓐ You really helped me out! Thank you for telling me the important news.
你真的幫了我！謝謝你告訴我這重要的消息。

Ⓑ Not at all. It's a piece of cake.
別客氣。這只是小事一樁。

字　彙

auto factory 修車廠

Chapter 5

表達否定、拒絕或命令之意用語

327. Don't be a stranger.

（161）

別裝不熟。

說　明

　　當你和某人認識或相處一段時間後，卻要分離時，就可以用上這句話，表示即使分別後，也別疏於聯絡或是裝不熟。

情境對話1：

Ⓐ Hey! Don't be a stranger, ok?
　　嘿！別裝不熟，好嗎？

Ⓑ I know. I will write you an e-mail.
　　我知道。我會寫電子郵件給你。

情境對話2：

Ⓐ We're going to graduate this June. I feel so upset.
　　我們今年六月就要畢業了。我覺得好難過。

Ⓑ It's ok, but don't be a stranger.
　　沒關係，但別疏於聯絡。

字　彙

stranger 陌生人

328. Don't be so childish.

別幼稚了。

說　明

　　當你的友人所做出的事情或想法讓你覺得很不成熟，或還是像小孩子般那麼幼稚時，就可以跟他說這句話，也類似 Grow up!這句話。

情境對話1：

Ⓐ Don't be so childish, Mark. You are 30 years old.
別幼稚了，馬克。你已經三十歲了。

Ⓑ But I really want to go to Disneyland.
但我真的想去迪士尼樂園。

情境對話2：

Ⓐ If Iris doesn't participate in the play, I won't, either.
如果艾莉絲不參加這場戲的演出，我也不要參加。

Ⓑ Don't be so childish, ok?
別幼稚了，好嗎？

字　彙

Disneyland 迪士尼樂園　　　participate 參加

---

329. Don't be so mean!

別太尖酸刻薄。

說　明

若你的友人或同事、家人講話太直接或尖酸刻薄以至於中傷別人時，就可以用這句話告訴對方。

情境對話1：

Ⓐ Don't be so mean to your younger brother, Gary!
蓋瑞，別對你的弟弟太尖酸刻薄！

Ⓑ But he is very naughty and always takes my things without my permission.
但他非常調皮而且總是沒經過我的允許就拿走我的東西。

情境對話2：

Ⓐ I wish that she had never come to this world.
我希望她從未來到這世上。

Ⓑ Don't be so mean. At least, she is your family.
別這麼尖酸刻薄。至少，她是你的家人。

字　彙

mean　卑鄙的；吝嗇的

330. Don't beat around the bush.

別拐彎抹角。

說　明

有些人講話比較會拐彎抹角，或是繞一大圈，或是話有絃外之音，讓人摸不著頭緒或不清楚重點時，就可以用這句話告訴對方，表示有話就直說，別拐彎抹角。

情境對話1：

Ⓐ Sir, I have something to tell you but I'm not sure if this is an appropriate time now...
長官，我有事要跟你說，但我不確定現在是否是恰當的時機……

Ⓑ Don't beat around the bush. Just tell me directly.
別拐彎抹角。直接告訴我。

情境對話2：

Ⓐ Jason, don't beat around the bush.
傑森，別拐彎抹角。

Ⓑ Ok, then. Could you please lend me fifty thousand dollars to pay the loan?
好，那麼。你可以借我五萬元來償還貸款嗎？

字 彙

appropriate 適宜的　　　　　　　directly 直接地

---

331. Don't fall for it!

別上當!

說 明

　當你發現某件事情事有蹊蹺時，或是某人的意圖是不懷好意或心懷不軌，讓你識破其計謀時，就可以用這句話警惕對方，不要輕易上當。

情境對話1：

Ⓐ Jason wanted to invite me to his cottage.
傑森想邀請我到他的小木屋。

Ⓑ Don't fall for it! He is very tricky.
別上當！他是個很狡猾的人。

情境對話2：

Ⓐ If any stranger asks your phone number or address, don't fall for it!
如果有任何陌生人要你的電話號碼或是地址，別上當！

Ⓑ Thank you for telling me such essential information.
謝謝你告訴我這麼重要的資訊。

字 彙

cottage 小木屋；農舍

tricky 狡猾的

essential 重要的

332. Don't fish in troubled water.

別混水摸魚。

說 明

這句話最常用在工作的場合，尤其是上位管理階層者常對屬下說這句話。另外，當你看不下你的友人整天無所事事，或是沒有專心致力於某件事情上，反而做與正事無關的事情時，也可以用此句提醒、勸戒他。

情境對話1：

A Don't fish in troubled water.
別混水摸魚了。

B Ok, I'll go fix the car now.
好，我現在就修車去。

情境對話2：

A Mom, I'm going out with my friends and will come back later.
媽，我要跟朋友出去，待會就回來。

B Don't fish in troubled water. Go to sweep the backyard immediately.
別混水摸魚了。立刻去清掃後院。

字 彙

backyard 後院

immediately 立即；馬上

333. Don't judge a person by his appearance.

(164)

別以貌取人。

說　明

　大部分的人都會因為外表或第一印象來論斷他人，但真正要了解一個人，是要藉由相處與溝通後才能漸漸認識此人的個性或想法。所以當你的友人只憑外觀就來評斷對一個人的喜惡時，就可以告訴他這句話。

情境對話1：

Ⓐ Look! That man looks so awful and with a ragged coat. I think he must be a beggar.
看！那個男人看起來很糟而且又穿件破爛的外套。我想他一定是乞丐。

Ⓑ Don't judge a person by his appearance.
別以貌取人。

情境對話2：

Ⓐ Don't judge a person by his appearance for it might give us a misunderstanding of a person.
別以貌取人，因為如此一來可能會讓我們誤解一個人。

字　彙

ragged　破爛的；衣衫襤褸的

beggar　乞丐

misunderstanding　誤解；誤會

334. Don't let me down.

> 別讓我失望。

說　明

　　當你倚賴對方或期許對方能有不錯的表現時，就可以用這句話告訴他，對方就有可能因此受到肯定而盡力達成目標。但有時也會是某種程度的壓力。這裡的 down 是指 "失望" 的意思。

情境對話1：

Ⓐ Our preparation work is almost done.
籌備工作已差不多完成。

Ⓑ Ok. I'll look forward to hearing some good news. Don't let me down.
好。我期待能聽到好消息。別讓我失望。

情境對話2：

Ⓐ You are the only hope of this village. Don't let me down.
你是這村裡唯一的希望。別讓我失望。

Ⓑ I know. I'll do my best.
我知道。我會盡全力的。

字　彙

village 村子

335. Don't look at me like that.

> 別那樣看著我。

說　明

　　當你覺得對方看你的眼光有別於以往，或是有輕視、鄙棄，覺得你很奇怪的意味時，諸如此類的異樣眼光讓你感到不舒服時，就可以用這句話告訴對方。

情境對話1：

Ⓐ Don't look at me like that. I'm not the only one who made the mistake.
別那樣看我。我又不是唯一做錯事的人。

Ⓑ I know. I just feel curious.
我知道。我只是感到好奇而已。

情境對話2：

Ⓐ Were you the last one who left the music classroom last night?
昨晚你是最後一個離開音樂教室的人嗎？

Ⓑ No, I wasn't. Don't look at me like that.
不，我不是。別那樣看我。

字　彙

curious 好奇的

336. Don't look down on me.

別看不起我。

說　明

當你覺得對方表現出有輕視或看不起你的意味時，就可以用這句話告訴他。而 me 可以換成其他人。

情境對話1：

Ⓐ We shouldn't look down on people whose academic background is lower than us.
我們不應該看不起學歷背景比我們低的人。

Ⓑ That's right!
沒錯！

情境對話2：

Ⓐ Don't look down on me just because I'm poor.
別因為我窮而看不起我。

Ⓑ I don't. I never think that.
我沒有。我從未有這種想法。

字　彙

academic 學術的　　　　　　　background 背景

---

337. Don't make fun of me.

別開我玩笑。

說　明

　有的人很喜歡開玩笑，以緩和緊張的氣氛，或是帶來歡樂的氣氛，但不管如何，開玩笑總是要有個限度，倘若有人開的玩笑讓你感覺很不舒服，或是使你有被嘲笑或歧視的感覺時，就可以用這句話回應，提醒對方別再繼續開你的玩笑。

情境對話1：

Ⓐ Don't make fun of me!
別開我玩笑了！

Ⓑ Sorry, but your new haircut is "so fashionable".
對不起，但是你的新髮型實在是"太時髦"了。

情境對話2：

Ⓐ Hey, what's wrong with your voice? It sounds so weird and funny.
嘿，你的聲音怎麼了？聽起來很怪又好笑。

Ⓑ Don't make fun of me. I just got a bad cold yesterday.
別開我玩笑了。我昨晚才重感冒。

字　彙
fashionable　時髦的；流行的

338. **Don't move!**

不准動！

說　明

此句有很多種用法，需視情境或上下文而定。例如：警察捉壞人時會用上這句話；旁邊有危險物品或是動物時，也可以用這句話警告他人；或是不要移動該當事者的個人所有物……等等。

情境對話1：

Ⓐ Don't move! There is a lion behind you. Just walk slowly and gently.
不要動！你背後有一隻獅子。放慢腳步並輕輕地走。

Ⓑ Ok!
好！

情境對話2：

Ⓐ Walter, your bedroom is like a pigpen, especially the closet. I can't take it anymore.
瓦特，你的臥室就像個豬圈似的，尤其是你的衣櫥。我再也受不了了。

Ⓑ Don't move anything! I'll clean them later.
都不要動！我待會會清理。

字　彙
behind　在~後面　　　　　gently　輕輕地；和緩地
pigpen　豬舍；髒亂的地方

339. Don't waste your breath.

167

別浪費力氣了。

說　明

有些人一旦下了決心，就不會輕易更改其決定或想法，或是本身個性就很固執的人，就算旁人費盡口舌，他們也不會有所動搖時，就可以用這句話告訴那些想要勸說這樣個性的人的朋友，別浪費力氣了。

情境對話1：

Ⓐ Don't waste your breath. He won't easily change his mind.
別浪費力氣了。他不會輕易更改他的決定。

Ⓑ Yeah. Larry is stubborn.
是啊。賴瑞的個性是很固執的。

情境對話2：

Ⓐ I need to convince her to stay.
我要說服她留下來。

Ⓑ Don't waste your breath. She has made up her mind.
別浪費力氣了。她已經下定決心了。

字　彙

stubborn 倔強、固執的　　　convince 說服

340. I'm not interested.

我沒興趣。

說　明

當對方想邀你從事某項活動，但你沒有興趣，或不想加入但又不好意思直接拒絕時，就可以用這句話委婉地表示拒絕。

情境對話1：

Ⓐ What do you think about this election?
你對次的選舉有什麼想法？

Ⓑ Uh. I'm not interested in politics.
呃。我對政治沒有興趣。

情境對話2：

Ⓐ I told you that I'm not interested in comedies.
我告訴過你我對喜劇沒有興趣。

Ⓑ But the plot of this film is really attractive.
但這部電影的劇情真的很引人入勝。

字　彙

politics 政治	comedy 喜劇
plot 情節；密謀、計畫	film 電影
attractive 有吸引力的	

341. I'm not sure I can do it.

這事我恐怕做不了。

說　明

當對方邀你從事某項活動時，但你可能因為有事在身，或是其實你很想參與，但卻怕力有未逮時，就可以用這句話表示。

情境對話1：

Ⓐ I'm not sure I can do it. It's too adventurous.
這事我恐怕做不了。這太冒險了。

Ⓑ Come on! You can do it!
來嘛！你可以的！

情境對話2：

Ⓐ Do you want to see the opera tonight?
你今晚想看去歌劇嗎？

Ⓑ Well, I'm not sure I can do it. I have a test tomorrow.
呃，我恐怕不行。我明天要考試。

字　彙
adventurous 冒險的　　　　opera 歌劇

342. I can't afford it.

我負擔不起。

說　明
當你所想買的物品，或是別人想要你買的東西，其價錢是超過你能負擔的金錢時，就可以用這句話表示。

情境對話1：

Ⓐ Dad, I want that sports car. It looks so cool.
爸，我想要那輛跑車。它看起來好酷。

Ⓑ Son, even if I work until I'm 80 years old, I still can't afford it.
兒子，即使我工作到八十歲，我還是買不起那輛跑車。

情境對話2：

Ⓐ Sorry, I can't afford it. It's too expensive.
抱歉，我負擔不起。這太貴了。

Ⓑ That's ok. You can pay it in twelve installments.
沒關係。你可以分十二期來付款。

字　彙
sports car 跑車　　　　afford 負擔
installment 分期付款

343. I can't help it.　⟨169⟩

> 我沒辦法。

說　明

　當你碰上某些讓你無法克制自己情緒或行為的事情時，例如：最愛的美食、可愛的動物或是討厭的人事物，或是難以改變的習性時，但別人想要你克制一下或改變時，你就可以用上這句話。

情境對話1：

🅐 I can't help it when I see or smell the delicious food.
幫我看見或聞到美食的時候，我就克制不住。

🅑 Me, too. They always attract me to have them.
我也是。它們總是吸引我去品嚐它們。

情境對話2：

🅐 Can you control yourself? Don't be so hasty.
你可以控制一下嗎？別這麼急急忙忙。

🅑 I can't help it. I just want things done within a short time.
我沒辦法。我就是想要在短時間內完成事情。

字　彙

attract 吸引　　　　　　　　hasty 倉促、急忙的
within 在～範圍內

344. I can't wait!

> 我已經等不及了！

說　明

　有時候，我們對於心中所期待的事情真的實現時，而迫不及待想親眼見證或體驗時，例如：喜愛的國外歌手到自己的國家開演唱會，或是某個比賽或考試的結果就要揭曉時，讓人緊張、興奮又期待時，就可以用這句話表示心中難以掩飾的情緒。

情境對話1：

Ⓐ I can't wait to see my newborn baby!
我已經等不及要看我剛出生的小寶貝！

Ⓑ Me, too. I think she must be adorable.
我也是。我想她一定很可愛。

情境對話2：

Ⓐ Do you know Brad Pete will come to Taiwan tomorrow to promote his new movie?
你知道布來德‧彼特明天要來台宣傳他的新作嗎？

Ⓑ Really? Oh, I can't wait to see him in person!
真的嗎？噢，我等不及要親眼見他了！

字　彙

adorable 可愛的；值得崇拜的 promote 宣傳

in person 親自

345. I decline.   170

我拒絕。

說　明

當你的友人邀請你參加某個活動，但你因事而無法參加時，或是要求你幫他一個忙，但你不想幫他時，可能是愛莫能助，或者這個忙也許會造成你的困擾、麻煩時，也或是有其他苦衷等因素時，就可以用上這句話以示拒絕。

情境對話1：

Ⓐ I declined the increase on my salary that my boss was going to give me.
我拒絕我老闆本來要給我的加薪。

B Are you insane? Why didn't you accept that?
你腦袋有問題啊？你怎麼不接受呢？

情境對話2：

A Miranda, can you pretend to be my wife in front of my parents?
米蘭達，你可以在我父母面前假裝是我妻子嗎？

B No. I decline. Why me?
不。我拒絕。為什麼是我？

字　彙

increase 增加　　　　　　insane 神智不清的；瘋狂的

---

346. I didn't mean it.

我不是故意的。

說　明

人總是會犯錯，但有時是不小心或無意的，此時就可以用這句話表示，如果真的是無意犯錯的話。

情境對話1：

A Why did you hit your younger sister?
你為什麼打你妹妹？

B I didn't mean it. She ran to me and bumped into me.
我不是故意的。是她自己跑向我然後撞到我。

情境對話2：

A I didn't mean it, Sandy. Please forgive me!
珊迪，我不是故意的。請你原諒我！

B It's too late. Your apology doesn't mean anything to me.
太遲了。你的道歉對我而言沒有任何意義。

字　彙

bump into 碰撞

永續圖書
線上購物網

www.foreverbooks.com.tw

◆ 加入會員即享活動及會員折扣。

◆ 每月均有優惠活動，期期不同。

◆ 新加入會員三天內訂購書籍不限本數金額，

  即贈送精選書籍一本。（依網站標示為主）

專業圖書發行、書局經銷、圖書出版

永續圖書總代理：

五觀藝術出版社、培育文化、棋茵出版社、大拓文化、讀
品文化、雅典文化、知音人文化、手藝家出版社、璞申文
化、智學堂文化、語言鳥文化

活動期內，永續圖書將保留變更或終止該活動之權利及最終決定權。

每日一句生活英語

雅致風靡　典藏文化

親愛的顧客您好，感謝您購買這本書。

為了提供您更好的服務品質，煩請填寫下列回函資料，您的支持
是我們最大的動力。

您可以選擇傳真、掃描或用本公司準備的免郵回函寄回，謝謝。

姓名：		性別：	□男　　□女
出生日期：　　年　　月　　日		電話：	
學歷：		職業：	□男　　□女
E-mail：			
地址：□□□			
從何得知本書消息：□逛書店　□朋友推薦　□DM廣告　□網路雜誌			
購買本書動機：□封面　□書名□排版　□內容　□價格便宜			
你對本書的意見： 內容：□滿意□尚可□待改進　　編輯：□滿意□尚可□待改進 封面：□滿意□尚可□待改進　　定價：□滿意□尚可□待改進			
其他建議：			

總經銷：永續圖書有限公司

永續圖書線上購物網
www.foreverbooks.com.tw

您可以使用以下方式將回函寄回。

您的回覆，是我們進步的最大動力，謝謝。

① 使用本公司準備的免郵回函寄回。

② 傳真電話：（02）8647-3660

③ 掃描圖檔寄到電子信箱：

yungjiuh@ms45.hinet.net

沿此線對折後寄回，謝謝。

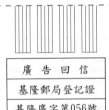

| 廣 告 回 信 |
| 基隆郵局登記證 |
| 基隆廣字第056號 |

2 2 1 - 0 3

雅典文化事業有限公司　收
新北市汐止區大同路三段194號9樓之1

雅致風靡　典藏文化